BERNARD LAZARE

THE GATE OF IVORY

TRANSLATED AND WITH AN INTRODUCTION BY
BRIAN STABLEFORD

THIS IS A SNUGGLY BOOK

ISBN: 978-1-64525-027-2

THE GATE OF IVORY

BERNARD LAZARE (1865–1903) was a French Jewish literary critic and journalist. Though mostly remembered today for his prominent role in the Dreyfus Affair and his book *Antisemitism: Its History and Causes*, he was also an important member of the Symbolist movement, and one of its purest and most extravagant exponents. He wrote drama and some poetry, but the core of his production consisted of an extensive sequence of short stories, or elaborated poems in prose, most of which he published in Symbolist periodicals between 1887 and 1893, and which he subsequently organized into three augmented collections. Although somewhat neglected today, for reasons that have nothing to do with their literary and philosophical merit, Lazare's short stories are key documents of the Symbolist movement, and a remarkable illustration of the methods and preoccupations of the writers whose activity constituted its heyday.

BRIAN STABLEFORD'S scholarly work includes *New Atlantis: A Narrative History of Scientific Romance* (Wildside Press, 2016), *The Plurality of Imaginary Worlds: The Evolution of French roman scientifique* (Black Coat Press, 2017) and *Tales of Enchantment and Disenchantment: A History of Faerie* (Black Coat Press, 2019). In support of the latter projects he has translated more than a hundred volumes of *roman scientifique* and more than twenty volumes of *contes de fées* into English.

His recent fiction, in the genre of metaphysical fantasy, includes a trilogy of novels set in West Wales, consisting of *Spirits of the Vasty Deep* (2018), *The Insubstantial Pageant* (2018) and *The Truths of Darkness* (2019), published by Snuggly Books..

Contents

Introduction

L A PORTE D'IVOIRE by Bernard Lazare, here translated as *The Gate of Ivory*, was first published by Armand Colin et Cie in an edition dated 1897, but actually published in 1898. It was issued shortly after *Les Porteurs de torches* (1897; tr. in a Snuggly Books edition as *The Torch-Bearers*) and had probably been submitted to the publisher at the same time, having been prepared in parallel with it. Most of the stories making it up, however, must have been published some time before the compilation of the latter volume, perhaps overlapping the publication of the items contained in the author's first short story collection, *Le Miroir des légendes* (1892; tr. as *The Mirror of Legends* in a Snuggly Books edition of 2017).

Although there is an obvious continuity between the stories assembled in *Le Miroir des légendes* and those collected in *La Porte d'Ivoire*, there is also an evident evolution in both their narrative method and their contextual packaging. The stories in *La Porte d'Ivoire* are supplied, tacitly if not explicitly, with an active narrator named Anselme who frequently comments on the stories, routinely using them to illustrate the philosophical pontifications to which he seems to be addicted. The collection is introduced by a dialogue between Anselme and his friend Nalle, who also features in many of the stories as a listener to whom their narration is addressed, either individually or as a member of a group.

That device adds a layer of complication to the stories in *La Porte d'Ivoire* that, while by no means unusual as a method employed in French literary portmanteaux, is rarely employed with such earnest intensity. Embedding stories within stories in that fashion moves into the foreground of the reading experience the question of the functions of storytelling, ranging from the fundamental reason why stories exist at all to sophisticated analyses of the nutritional value of the food for thought that they contain. In doing that, *La Porte d'Ivoire* is closely linked to *Les Porteurs de torches*, which raises such questions more forthrightly and addresses them more directly. *La Porte d'Ivoire* is a more diffuse and varied work than its companion, but, precisely for that reason, it is more far-ranging and more subtle.

In consequence, *La Porte d'Ivoire* reads very well in isolation, but it benefits considerably from being read in partnership with its immediate predecessor, although it is quite a different animal in terms of its narrative binding and its political propagandizing. While *Les Porteurs de torches* displays the author's Anarchist sympathies more extravagantly than almost any other work of fiction produced at a time when the majority of the Parisian literary *avant garde* professed such sympathies, *La Porte d'Ivoire* develops a much more general subversive skepticism, and a greater finesse in its deployment of challenges to orthodox thought. It lacks the stylistic flamboyance that had made *La Miroir des légendes* one of the archetypal prose works of the Symbolist Movement's heyday, but the tightening of its style gives it a clearer focus, and gives its rhetoric a clarity and neatness that seems more sophisticated as well as more polished.

Although Lazare's three volumes of fiction have many things in common, therefore, and are obviously the work of the same mind, they are also quite distinct, each having its own personality, and even possessed of an element of sibling rivalry. That competition becomes particularly obvious in the way that *Les Porteurs de torches* deals with its own character named Anselme, who is an obvious analogue of, although not identical to, the hypothetical narrator featured in *Le Porte d'Ivoire*. There is a temptation to regard *La Porte d'Ivoire* as a progressive advancement on *La Miroir des légendes*, but that would be unfair to the earlier work, and all three volumes are better regarded as different facets of the author's literary personality, looking in different directions with the aid of different attitudes, making up a varied but integral set.

The Snuggly Books edition of *The Mirror of Legends* contains an overall account of Bernard Lazare's life and career, and a briefer synopsis was offered in the introduction to *The Torch-Bearers*, the substance of which it is worth repeating here. He was born Lazare Bernard on 14 June 1865 in Nîmes in the south of France, and went to Paris in October 1886 at the behest of his friend Georges Michel, who had preceded him there in 1883. Michel was part of Stéphane Mallarmé's circle of acolytes, who formed the core of the burgeoning Symbolist Movement, and who published poetry and prose as Ephraïm Mikhail; he and Lazare became the central figures of a subsidiary clique. Lazare soon joined one of the Movement's other key *cénacles*, the salon hosted by José-Maria de Heredia, and he also met and befriended the aged Comte de Villiers de l'Isle Adam, now fallen on hard times but a legendary hero to young writers of "Decadent literature"—a description initially coined as an insult aimed at Romantic writers, but adopted with pride by the more radical practitioners of literary *romanticisme*, assertively retained by several of the promoters of post-Romantic *avant gardes* and worn with particular pride by many of the Symbolists.

Lazare's position at the heart of the Symbolist Movement retained his wholehearted commitment for a number of years; he published prolifically in Symbolist periodicals between 1887 and 1893, when all of the material in *Le Miroir des Légendes* and at least some of the material in *La Porte d'Ivoire* was written. His literary activity was already broadening out, however, by virtue of political and philosophical interests that he only shared with a minority of his fellow Symbolists—a tiny minority in respect of his strong interest in the history and cultural situation of Judaism, which became even tinier when Georges Michel died of tuberculosis in 1890. Superficially, the interest taken by one sector of the Movement in the philosophy of Anarchism seemed a much larger minority but in fact, the appellation was often a casual affectation. In Lazare's case, it was not; his numerous journalistic contributions to Anarchist periodicals showed a rare intellectual commitment and analytical fervor, of which *Les Porteurs de torches* was the most elaborate fruit.

The first major product of Lazare's interest in Judaism was his analytical history of *L'Antisémitisme, son histoire et ses causes* (1894; tr. as *Anti-Semitism, its History and its Causes*), whose attempts to explain the phenomenon seemed to some readers to be lending fuel to it, and led to continual repetition of the absurd charge that Lazare was himself anti-semitic—an accusation that continued to haunt his reputation for the rest of his life and long after his death. That interest was central to Lazare's major political involvement, which began when he wrote an article in 1896 castigating the shabby treatment meted out by the French army and the French political establishment to the ill-fated Captain Alfred Dreyfus, the victim of an ugly injustice. Lazare's article ended with the ringing phrase "J'accuse," subsequently employed as a headline by Émile Zola, and effectively launched the so-called "Dreyfus Affair," which raged in Paris for the next decade.

The fact that Lazare published no more fiction after 1898 probably had more to do with his intense involvement in campaigning on behalf of Dreyfus than the after-effect of the disillusionments measured and specified in *Les Porteurs de Torches*. He died before the Affair was concluded, on 1 September 1903, following surgery that attempted to remove a malignant tumor from his bowel. There were, however, other complicating factors in his life that limited his literary production after 1892. In that year he married Isabelle Grumbach, with whom he had been romantically linked since they had met in Nîmes as teenagers, and who had followed him to Paris, supporting herself there by working in Nadar's photographic studio. His family had always opposed the relationship; they refused to attend the wedding and effectively cut him off thereafter, surrounding the couple with a hostility to which Lazare always reacted defiantly. The stories in *La Porte d'Ivoire*, like all of Lazare's fiction, exhibit a particular defensive tension and equivocation in their attitude to amour that distinguishes his dealings with that topic from other Symbolist treatments of the subject.

It is unsurprising that Lazare chose to lead off his collection with a "Dialogue" in which Anselme attempts to justify the diversity of its contents in a conversation with his favorite sounding-board, his friend Nalle, nor is it surprising that the argument is a trifle disingenuous in selecting out that diversity as the aspect of the collection most in need of apologetic defense. The selection of "Le Triomphe de l'amour" ("The Triumph of Love") to lead off the collection is both appropriate and somewhat provocative, as it provides a particularly stark example, not only of the unusual narrative strategy of the stories, routinely involving hypothetical verbal narrations as illustrations of arguments put forward by specified narrators—in this case supplied with a third layer by the superimposition of Anselme external to the professor of philosophy—but also of the laconic iconoclasm of their concluding judgments.

In that ironic layering, the stories are closely allied with the strong French traditions of *contes cruels*, which received a tremendous boost in the *fin-de-siècle* period because of their methodical mass production for newspaper feuilleton slots. That adaptation routinely subjected them to a spatial straitjacket, confining their word-length to a narrow span of approximately 1,400-1,800 words. Lazare undoubtedly took lessons in method from some of the other writers who became expert in adapting their work to such slots, including Catulle Mendès, Jean Richepin, Léon Bloy and Octave Mirbeau, but he also developed an idiosyncratic expertise of his own, whose application is obvious throughout the collection.

Lazare certainly did not scorn the kind of buoyantly sarcastic humor that became typical of the *conte cruel* format, which is displayed with particular effectiveness here in "La Confession de Don Juan" ("The Confession of Don Juan") and "La Future de Prospero" ("Prospero's Flight"), nor did he neglect the invaluable resource of colorful erotic perversity, frankly displayed in such stories as "Le Suprême baiser" ("The Supreme Kiss") and the subsection of the final item in the collection entitled "Le Mort des eaux" ("The Death of the Waters"), but his greatest cleverness in donning the straitjacket was the economical complexity of his carefully-embedded narratives, which few of his rivals could match. When he took up conventional themes and motifs that were routinely developed in the genre—Don Juan, Salome, the Wandering Jew, vengeful apparitions, case-studies from the asylum, etc.—he not only succeeded in adding new twists to their familiar denouements but also in adding a transformative labyrinthine quality to their narration.

Although there is a sense, therefore, in which the stories in *La Porte d'Ivoire* are more deliberately commercialized work than those in *Le Miroir des légendes*, and certainly more so than the propagandistic elements making up *Les Porteurs de torches*, they are no less elegant and no less serious. The introductory dialogue deliberately refers to the use of the Homeric metaphor of the Gate of Ivory as a title, pointing out that the gate in question is supposedly the source of deceptive dreams, whereas "true" dreams emerge from the Gate of Horn, but calls attention thereby to the element of double bluff in the manner in which the metaphor has very often been employed in literature.

As a lover of legend, Lazare would have been well aware of the fact that it was through the Gate of Ivory that Homer's most enthusiastic acolyte, Virgil, brought Aeneas back from the Underworld—the description of which became the basis of Dante's vision of the Inferno—precisely because its deceptions are sometimes innately truer than the tedious landscapes glimpsed through the Gate of Horn. That is, in a nutshell, the whole point of the multilayered stores in *La Porte d'Ivoire*: that the complex filtration of fiction by the imagination might be an essentially deceptive process, but that if it is done well, the filtrate has a purity that mere reflection of quotidian observation cannot match.

This translation was made from the copy of the Armand Colin edition reproduced on the Bibliothèque Nationale's gallica website.

—Brian Stableford

THE GATE OF IVORY

Dialogue

"WHAT will you call this book?" asked Nalle.[1]

"I will call it, if you please, *The Gate of Ivory*," replied Anselme.

"Why?"

"Because all these tales, which I have told, are as various as the dreams that haunt us and the thoughts that assail us."

"However, your stories are melancholy or tragic, and the dreams there have more often passed through the Gate of Horn than the Gate of Ivory."

"You are only judging thus by virtue of lack of reflection. Do you not think that I have experienced more joy than sadness in dreaming my dreams? They have sometimes been a living commentary on my ideas; at other times they have engendered them; often, I have attempted to objectify a few ideologies within them, in order to make them more gripping, and to allow their consequences or their scope to be seen more clearly; and on certain evenings, they have been the friends of my solitude, and have populated it."

---

1 Nalle, Finnish for "bear," is frequently used there as a nickname for people named Björn, that being the equivalent word in Swedish.

"Is that sufficient to give a unity to your book?"

"Do you find the sequence of evocations incoherent? Is that because of the mixture of the ancient and modern, and the facility with which my dreams vagabond from Antioch in the eighth century to Spain in the Middle Ages, the Rome of the Borgias and our time?"

"I readily admit that the union of the present, quivering with life, with the past, the death of which horrifies me, is one of the causes of my disturbance."

"You're truly only stopping at the appearance of things. Tell me, what does it matter that I have placed modern ideas in the minds of heroes belonging to times that appear dead to you? Notice that I have carefully left aside the skeleton of those bygone ages—which is to say, their archeology. I have brought all those people, who are our ancestors, together, and I have brought them closer to certain contemporary souls who suffer the yoke of the same passions and thus know the power of similar ideas. That is why it ought to be of scant importance that the tales are modern and ancient by turns. Have I convinced you?"

"I'll tell you when I've read the pages that I've only heard."

"Read them seeking there the resemblances that make them children of the same mind. You'll see that their supreme unity lies in the very mind that conceived them, and which expresses therein the various aspects of a few ideas. And I'll write a conclusion for you that will doubtless persuade you, and enable you to comprehend more fully the past that you don't understand."

"So this book, although told to others, is written for me?"

"It is written for the mind that is my friend."

The Triumph of Love

IN accordance with his custom, after the dinner that
brought them together every week, Anselme spoke:

"I once knew an old professor of philosophy," he
said, "a very straight-thinking man, above all very logical, who seemed to take pleasure in contradicting his
thoughts by means of his actions. He had no peer in
debates; he knew how to depart from reliable principles
and to deduce irrefutable consequences therefrom; and
people derived great profit from his speech, if they
consented not to examine his actions. He preached an
austere morality and his existence was the most profli-
gate in the world; he was able to expose all the dangers
of drunkenness, but he was never as persuasive as when
wine had gone to his head; similarly, he spoke perfectly
about the deadly influence of women, but he found
his most convincing theorems and his most seductive
axioms in places of debauchery, when he had clearly
demonstrated the fragility of his senses.

"He explained his contradictions by denying human liberty and, nourished on the marrow of Spinoza
and fortified by the spirit of Schopenhauer, he had no
shortage of good reasons to explain his weaknesses and

those of humanity. He had undertaken a great work against free will, in which he showed that a man is the plaything of the most infimal causes and accidents, independent of his vain will. In that work he studied the most characteristic and the most notorious individuals, those he called the voluntarists, and he took them above all at their debut, wanting to prove that their vocation had always been determined by the god Hazard, all-powerful in directing souls while leaving them the illusion of guiding themselves.

"He had allowed me to leaf through his unfinished manuscript. It was enriched by numerous and curious anecdotes, all very ancient, since the most recent was that of Saint Paul on the road to Damascus, and I obtained an extreme childish pleasure in that reading.

"The professor of philosophy died a long time ago, of indigestion, some said, of a congestion caused by drunkenness or the abuse of women, affirmed others. He left me his work, not to publish, but in order to extract the most touching stories and entertain my friends with them. I shall follow his desire and tell you the first this evening. In reporting it I shall scrupulously conserve the style and manner of my dead friend."

Before the ascetic Candilya astonished India, and later the world, with his unusual austerities—it is said that he remained without any nourishment for six months, standing on the heel of his right foot with his left foot lodged in his loins—he was one of the most joyful princes that the divine Ganges had ever seen. He took pleasure in the society of courtesans, did not detest fermented beverages, gorged himself on meats, perhaps forbidden, and indulged in gambling, in spite of the remonstrations of the Brahmins who had watched over his childhood. In spite of the license of his mores, Candilya had a cultivated mind, he loved learning, and he held science in great esteem, considering her as the only goddess capable of giving happiness, by making the truth known.

After a few years of an idle life, wearied by futile pleasures and eager to develop his intellect, he decided to travel, in order to listen to the lessons of the best philosophers, the most savant mathematicians and the most illustrious moralists. He remained absent for more than ten years, he visited all the countries in the world, and legend says that he went as far as the blessed isles that are in the north, the isles veiled with mist and circled by ice, in which people know happiness.

It is scarcely possible today for us to admit such an assertion, the most recent works having demonstrated irrefutably that those islands only ever existed in a few eccentric minds, but we can suppose that Candilya perceived one day in the mists, the shores of the isles of the Cassiterides,[1] now Great Britain, and that he listened to the lying tales of some Phoenician. We do not have the same reasons for denying the arrival of Candilya at the Pillars of Hercules, which are doubtless our modern Gibraltar.

---

1 The Cassiterides ["Tin islands" in Greek], were mentioned by Herodotus and various other classical writers, most of whom were uncertain as to whether or not they were imaginary.

At any rate, Candilya profited intelligently from his voyages. He visited the most celebrated schools, followed the most renowned lessons, and did not even disdain to listen to the opinions of a few strange black men dominant in distant tribes, in which it is permissible for us to recognize fetishist sorcerers, and perhaps Dahomeyans.

When Candilya returned to India, an immense reputation had preceded him. It was said that he was learned in all things, that he had penetrated the most mysterious arcana and that he could pronounce the name of the supreme essence in twenty languages, which demonstrated to the most incredulous that he knew it perfectly. So, in the towns through which he passed, everyone gathered around him in order to hear him speak.

With great benevolence, he narrated his adventures, described the countries that he had visited and delighted in details and anecdotes about the mores of the inhabitants. Doubtless he lied a little, for he affirmed that he had climbed a pretended mountain of solid gold guarded by a centenarian old man, which we have been obliged to relegate to the domain of fable, in view of the impossibility of localizing it geographically. However, as no one could check his boasts, so natural for a traveler, Candilya was accompanied everywhere by an attentive cortege, and poets sang his praises, carried away by their enthusiasm, and also the hope of being attached to Candilya's house—for that was the time when princes nourished poets, albeit frugally, and were paid in smoke and sound.

He was received in his native city as a hero, which caused the warriors—a race even more jealous than bards—to murmur. Those paltry sentiments did not stop anyone, and all the young men desirous of contemplating Prince Candilya and listening to his discourse invited him to a respectful feast. Candilya accepted, and the following day, on the bank of the river, he presided over the feast offered to him by his admirers and friends.

When the most tenacious appetites were appeased, Candilya was asked to speak. He did so with a good grace, although it put him in the obligation of telling again stories that he had already told a hundred times over. The guests paid the greatest attention to his marvelous stories; as they had credulous minds they did not doubt for a moment the mountains of gold, the sea of milk, the ape-men, the giants and the pygmies. They similarly admired the emerald ocean where the marine herds grazed, and they were not wrong, for the most positive of our navigators have seen the Sargasso Sea.

Nevertheless, those fables, which had enchanted the people, did not satisfy the most subtle of those who were fêting Candilya. They asked him at what philosophy he had arrived after that long absence and those long days of study. Candilya reflected momentarily, and then, summarizing his beliefs and his metaphysics, he declared that what he had retained most clearly from the lessons heard was that desire is at the origin of things, that love is both the first and most powerful of the gods, and that it is him alone that gives and sustains life.

People approved of Candilya and praised him for having arrived at such a beautiful conception; only one young man, the youngest of those who were there, shook his head disdainfully. Candilya perceived that, and interrogated him softly: "Why do you seem to be scornful of me?"

"Listen to this story," replied the young man. "It will be my response. The merchant Matanga had a daughter, Saranya, as beautiful as the dawn. He had promised her in marriage to Sambadar, who loved her, and whom she loved, and they both rejoiced at the thought of soon living together. But the devas take pleasure in testing humans. Sambadar departed for a long voyage, and his lover, desperate, paraded her chagrin through the gardens and the woods.

"One morning, when she was picking flowers and thinking about her beloved, she was bitten by a snake, and died pronouncing Sambadar's name. Matanga had her beautiful body burned, conserved the precious ashes in a jade vase, and presented them to Sambadar when he returned to look for his fiancée. Sambadar did not weep; he pressed the urn to his breast, and then he composed in honor of Kama a song of supplication and praise, and, when he finished, Saranya was resuscitated.

"That tale was told to me by an old woman who hunts the outskirts of the city," the young man concluded. "It made me understand that love is the highest of the gods, that it was the creator, and I had no need, in order to know that truth, to quit the banks of the Ganges . . ."

Then, Canilya was humiliated. He confessed the vanity of science and the futility of quitting the land where one has been born and nourished, in order to find the truth. He spent the night in prayer and, after being purified, the next day, he took off his garments and withdrew to the nearby forest in order to meditate on the truth.

"Thus," my philosopher concluded, "Candilya owed his sanctity to the words of an old woman, repeated by a child."

He also owed it to that circumstance that he was, in sum, a poor intelligence, for imbecility is the indispensable condition of sanctity.

If Candilya had had a more open mind he would have been able to reply to his young interlocutor that he had not heard mention of the egotistical and particular love celebrated by the old woman of the outlying district, but of the vast, profound, subtle and intelligent love that permits the knowledge, comprehension and service of humankind. But voyages could not teach Candilya anything, because Candilya was a simpleton, and he was born to believe that wisdom resides in the squealing of simple minds interpreted by sophists and mild skeptics, the philosophers of uncertainty—which is to say, the most vain and stupid of human beings.

That is why the sole effort of which that prince found himself capable, after years of reflection, was that of sticking his left foot in his crotch.

The Enigma

THE city of Antioch—this is not the Antioch that knew Christian preaching but an older, if not more famous, city unknown to the majority of geographers—was a very dissolute city. Its citizens placed chariot races above public affairs, preferred athletes to orators, combats with the cestus to those of rhetors and sophists, and rather than hear a discourse on virtue, they prefer to give themselves to vice. From dawn to dusk, the streets of the city resounded with the noise of songs; the sound of flutes was heard in closed houses in which the tables were set up at dawn, and in the streets one encountered corteges of youths crowned with roses and hyacinths following the gilded litters of courtesans. The courtesans were numerous; they were honored and they were loved, primarily because they were facile, and although it was not permitted for everyone to go to Corinth,[1] Antioch was open to all comers.

---

1 *Non licet omnibus adire Corinthum* [Not everyone is permitted to go to Corinth] was a popular saying in ancient Rome, where the idea of the ancient Greek city was irrevocably associated with the prostitutes of the Temple of Aphrodite, signifying that not everyone can afford to visit pretentious brothels.

At about the time of Alexander's death, approximately, King Kratis governed Antioch. Kratis was worthy of reigning over his people. Although a few white hairs were showing in his blond and delicately undulating beard, he could still measure himself against young men in all games. Once, his beauty, grace and strength had been celebrated, and poets had been able, without lying excessively, to compare him to Apollo and Heracles; with age, he had acquired majesty, and nowadays, when he was praised in dithyrambs, it was as similar to Zeus.

Kratis was a widower, but he did not regret his wife, the daughter of a neighboring king whom he had doubtless married for reasons of State. From his marriage he had four daughters, and he had already married three of them to friendly princes.

Those three princesses were beautiful, but the fourth, Lysis, surpassed them all, and when they were all together one might have thought her a swan in the middle of a flock of geese. Lysis drove painters and sculptors to despair; to describe her charms, calami were impotent; she maddened the drivers in the hippodrome, and more than one caused his chargers to drop dead at her feet; she troubled the young men in the stadium, and Polemon, the son of Pericles, having set eyes on her, was killed by a discus that he was unable to avoid. For her, the hetaerae were forgotten, and some of the latter had cut their hair as a sign of affliction.

As soon as Lysis was a woman, the best-born, richest and most handsome men asked Kratis for her hand.

Kratis responded at first that, Lysis being the youngest of his daughters, he could not allow her to marry before her elders. That reason appeared plausible to the inhabitants of Antioch, and they only understood its vanity when Lysis remained alone in the palace with her father, for Kratis still refused to allow her to marry. He alleged her youth, and also the delicacy and fragility of her beauty, which he did not want to expose to the inevitable vulgarities of marriage.

However, young men flocked to Antioch from all the corners of the world, and no woman since the victorious Helen had enchained as many slaves as Lysis. Attracted by the virgin's renown, they came from Rome and from the shore that Carthage had once dominated, the lands of Saba and Adiabene, Alexandria and Syracuse, Phocea, the pillars of Hercules and the India that Alexander conquered, and one day, a strange warrior even arrived from a misty and distant island situated beyond Gaul, of which a thousand fables were told.

Thus assailed, Kratis brought all his daughter's suitors together one day and spoke to them.

"You want Lysis," he said, "and truly, your number is such and your merits so various that choosing between you cannot help but embarrass me. Nevertheless, as it is time that the unrest provoked by your crews and your enterprises ended, I have made a decision today. To win a wife as accomplished as my daughter, it is necessary to run some danger. You could all bloody Antioch by fighting one another in single combat, but perhaps the ultimate victor would be so disfigured by his triumph that he would no longer be worthy of Lysis. It would be the same for the games of the palaestra, and there again, you seem to be of such equal strength that it would be difficult for the triumph of one among you to be determined. So, this is what I have decided. Let those who want Lysis for a wife and who want to conquer her even at the risk of death come to my palace tomorrow. There, I will propose an enigma to them; the man who is able to tear away its veils will be able to take my daughter out of the gynaeceum, but—and this is what I expect of all of you—those who do not find the key will perish by poison. I have spoken."

The next day, of the host of men, only twenty presented themselves to confront the ordeal; the others had quit Antioch at first light, for they held their life to be precious above all. Their caravans encumbered the roads, where Roman horses collided with the camels of Arab chieftains and the elephants of Hindu princes.

The twenty were introduced to the presence of Kratis, sitting on his throne with Lysis by his side. They were placed on ivory stools and the king posed the enigma to them in these terms.

"Near the city of Babylon in the time of the hero Kyros lived a gardener whose orchards were illustrious. A thousand trees of numerous species were gathered around his dwelling, and the aroma of their flowers was such that it perfumed the country. The gardener did not allow anyone but him to pick their fruits; he placed them in silver baskets and went to sell them in the city.

"Among those trees there was a marvelous orange tree; the gardener had planted it himself and it was said that it was born of an orange from the Hesperides. When it bore fruit, all the inhabitants of Babylon wanted to taste its fabulous golden apples; the gardener sold them one by one, but he carefully refrained from touching the one that crowned the highest branch of the tree. That one was incredibly large; its color caused all its companions to pale, and the odor that it spread was sufficient to intoxicate.

"The king wanted it, for he thought that it was worthy of him alone, and he sent his minister in quest of it; but the gardener did not want to let go of it, in spite of the gold and the dignities he was offered. The king, who was obstinate, gave the gardener three days, at the end of which he would perish if he did not bring the miraculous fruit to his sovereign.

"The gardener made no response, and when the three days had elapsed, the king sent his soldiers to put the rebellious subject to death and take possession of the coveted marvel. The soldiers invaded the garden by night, but the house was deserted. They searched the orchard, and at the foot of the tree they found the gardener's body. In his closed hand be held the orange, desiccated and also dead, for its master had expressed the juice."

When Kratis had spoken thus, he stood up, sent his daughter out and retired to a small room into which the suitors were led one by one. Beside Kratis, who was lying on a crimson bed, stood a slave who was holding a cup filled with poison. Nineteen came, and after having bowed to the king and having renounced the enigma, they drank the proffered cup without trembling.

When the twentieth came in, the marble paving-stones were strewn with cadavers.; he looked at them without paling. He was a Cretan who had no fortune of his own, but who had not forgotten the shepherd Paris. He was twenty years old and his name was Ephialtes. He saluted Kratis, leaned on a column and said: "King, I have divined the key."

"Speak," replied Kratis.

"This is it," said Ephialtes. "The gardener, O King, is you. The tree that you have planted is that of your family. The fruits that you have ceded voluntarily are your three daughters, and the golden apple, the queen of the others, is none other than Lysis. Neither for gold nor silver do you want to give her up, because she is for you the sovereign good. You will not put her in the hands of any young man because you have already taken her in yours; the juice that you have expressed is the perfume of her mouth, and you are an incestuous father."

Kratis did not respond for a few moments, his head bowed. Then he straightened up and replied: "You are right, Ephialtes, and you have penetrated the mystery; but since you have understood what the others were not able to understand, you will understand even better that Lysis cannot be yours. They died because they were impotent to pierce the mystery, and you will die for having conquered it."

"Give me the cup," said Ephialtes, "for it is truly the only thing that I want to receive from you henceforth."

So he said, and, having drunk, he went to join his rivals in death, while the impassive Kratis had Lysis summoned by the executioner.

Five-Sins

UNDER Valerius Diocletian Augustus, the son of Jupiter, a man who called himself Siba lived in Caesarea in Palestine.

Siba was a Jew, but a very bad Jew, for he rarely frequented the synagogues and was never seen with the doctors debating the law, or even listening to holy commentaries. Those of his coreligionists he frequented, and they were rare, did not esteem him greatly, and the most rigorous would not have eaten at his table, fearing pollution. In any case, most of them were unaware of the existence of that black sheep, and that scorn did not afflict Siba overmuch.

He was quite insouciant by nature, and thought more about satisfying his appetites than meriting the consideration of his fellow citizens. He had all the vices: he was a drunkard, quarrelsome, lustful, a glutton and idle, but he was only preoccupied with his passions in order to satisfy them, and only complained of their tyranny when his poverty prevented him from submitting to the beloved yoke. Siba had no scruples; had he lived in our day, our professors of virtue would have declared him deprived of moral sensibility. Because of that very unconsciousness, Siba was quite cheerful.

He was very popular among the Greeks and Syrians of the port; those rude men liked him because of his naïve frankness, but they were able to recognize their friend's faults, so they had nicknamed him Five-Sins; doubtless their simple minds had not conceived a sixth. Siba went with them to taverns to drink wine perfumed with resin and to eat little fried fish, for one last scruple forbade him meat. When Five-Sins was not drunk he worked, and the professions to which he devoted himself were as numerous as his vices.

Two years before the very sacred Emperor Diocletian retired to Salona in order to forget the cares of the throne by laboring the fields, a great drought desolated Caesarea. For six months the sky was implacable, and no benevolent cloud perfumed the air with its softness even temporarily. The country surrounding the city was parched and lamentable. The leaves on the trees withered under the sun's ardor; the soil split; it did not want to give fruits or vegetables, and only the vines on the hills seemed to enjoy that furnace.

Thus, every evening, haggard hordes of peasants came into Caesarea, and those starvelings yielded to the most legitimate of excesses when their impatience was refused the nourishment they required.

All supplications and appeals to the gods had been vain, and divinities were certainly numerous in Caesarea. The Greeks had invoked Zeus the rain-maker; the

Syrians had offered choice victims to Aphrodite; and the Christian priests had begged the crucified Nazarene whom they worshiped like a God.

The Jews were unable to remain indifferent to such a catastrophe. Many of their people were struck down; the porticoes of the synagogues became too narrow to contain the crowd of shepherds and laborers taking refuge there, and the rich dreaded having to nourish too many poor people.

Thus, Habbahue, an austere rabbi and savant doctor, who was the First of the Ancients of Israel, was obliged to tear himself away from the study and meditation of the Law, the sole occupation worthy of him, in order, in accord with Jehovah, to put an end to the evils afflicting his people.

Habbahue had known for a long time that it was sufficient, in order to obtain rain, for the most saintly member of the community to recite the prayers prescribed for times of drought. To determine that elect individual was evidently difficult, but Habbahue was fortunately convinced that the Almighty came to the aid of the ignorance of his faithful servants. He therefore looked around him, among those whose virtue was renowned.

He visited the old men who gave the better part of their time to charity, those who devoted their lives to caring for the sick, and the pious individuals who buried the dead after having had them purified in accordance with the rites. He even saw a doctor who had meditated for twenty years, without eating, on the mysterious reason that had impelled the Lord Sabahot to strike the Egyptians with ten plagues and only ten.

It was in vain. Before those men, Habbahue did not sense the celestial disturbance that would indicate the Anointed.

One morning, Habbahue, having become desperate, was sitting on his doorstep, reflecting on the fragility of consecrated virtues made of vanity and hypocrisy, thinking about the difficulty of finding a just man even among those who ornamented themselves with justice, pity, charity and love, when he thought he heard a voice that said to him: "Why haven't you seen Five-Sins?"

To that question, Habbahue replied that he had not seen Five-Sins because he did not know him; he was not even aware of his existence.

"Send for him, then," said the voice.

The old rabbi called his servant, Ruben, and asked him about the unknown Five-Sins.

"He's a man named Siba," Ruben replied, "whom the people of the port have nicknamed Five-Sins, because of his vices."

"It doesn't matter," said Habbahue. "Find him and bring him to me."

Ruben explored all the dives in Caesarea, and in the evening, he encountered Five-Sins in the company of a flute-player. He approached him with horror and acquitted his mission. Five-Sins was surprised by the honor that was being done to him by a person like Habbahue, but as he was vain and curious, he abandoned the flute-player—with whom he had been enjoying himself since the previous day, and of whom he was weary—and he went with Ruben.

The good servant took him to the doctor and withdrew discreetly.

Habbahue examined Five-Sins with attention and astonishment. Siba was a short thickset man with full and sensual lips, who reeked of wine and the perfume of vulgar make-up, which surprised Habbahue and even disgusted him. However, confident in the divine order, the rabbi mastered himself and interrogated Five-Sins.

"Your name is Siba?" he asked.

"Siba is my name, Rabbi," the little man replied, "but I'm more commonly known as Five-Sins, and I confess that I prefer the latter appellation."

"What is your profession, Five-Sins, since that's what you want to be called?"

"Go-between, Rabbi. I know all the courtesans in Caesarea, and, among the women, those who are only asking to weaken. I'm esteemed in that estate, for I'm honest; I've never cheated anyone, and I only take a small commission."

"Don't you have any other profession than that?"

"Yes, Rabbi; I clean the theater, I bring bathers their underwear and I amuse them while they're being massaged with my jokes and quips."

"You have, then, always served evil during your life?"

"So it's said," replied Five-Sins, modestly.

"Think, though. Have you never done good?"

"I don't really know what you mean, Rabbi," Five-Sins replied. "Listen, though. One day when I was wandering near the temple of Augustus I saw a woman sitting on the ground, who was lamenting and sobbing recklessly. Indifferent passers-by were bumping into her, but they didn't deign to look round, and without my help a heavily laden donkey would have injured her. I picked her up and asked the cause of her tears. She replied that her husband had been put in prison and that she couldn't procure the money demanded for the ransom, except by surrendering her body to a brothel-keeper.

"I don't know what sentiment came over me, Rabbi, but I, who know women, since I help them to debauch themselves, took pity on the despair of that one, who loved her husband to the point of not wanting to betray him. I wanted to help her; as I was poor. I sold my bed, my blanket and my stool, and thus having a sufficient sum, I gave it to the desolate woman so that she could ransom her husband without selling herself. Perhaps that's what you call doing good, Rabbi."

While Five-Sins was speaking, Habbahue sensed the spirit of God move him. So, when the little man had finished, he abandoned his seat and bowed. "You alone are worthy of praying for us in our distress, Five-Sins," he said to him.

That evening, having been washed clean of his pollutions in the synagogue, Five-Sins prayed for the salvation of all before the surprised Pharisees, and already, when he emerged from the house of prayer, clouds were covering the sky over Caesarea.

Habbahue felt a great joy in consequence; as an action of grace he recited the psalm in which it is said the Yahveh visits the earth and gives it abundance; and when he arrived at the line: "You relieve dryness with rain, you bless your seed," he wept with delight.

At the same moment, the Christian priests congratulated themselves for having touched the heart of Jesus, the pontiffs of Astarte and those of Zeus attributed to their prayers the glory of having convinced their divinities.

Only Siba did not attribute such great merit to himself; that same morning, an old mariner had announced the end of the dry spell, and Five-Sins only rejoiced in thinking about the imminent grape-harvest. When he felt the first drops of rain on his bare head he was satisfied by not having been deceived, and went to the port to look for the old mariner and have a drink with him.

The Virgin

THE monk Hierocas was a shrewd Greek, with a fine and cunning mind, who had embraced the monastic estate for the advantages it confers rather than the duties it imposes. As he was active in his humor, curious to see and to learn, sensible to the charms of the past without disdaining the beauties of the present, he had recoiled from the idea of retiring to a monastery and, envious of the glory of Hanno, Scylax of Caryanda, Pytheas of Massalia and Strabo, he had decided to explore the earth. At the age of twenty he had left Byzantium, his homeland, and for half a century he had traveled the world, from the Pillars of Hercules to the confines of Scythia, and from the isles of the Cassiterides, where tin is mined, to the land of the Seres.

When he reached the age of seventy, Hierocas ceased traveling and confined himself, never to emerge again, in his convent in Byzantium, which was placed under the special protection of John the Baptist. In spite of the fatigues of his existence, he was still robust and valiant, and he was counting on ten years of life in order to write the story of his voyages, which he wanted to render picturesque, lively and amiable, after the fashion of the *Periegesis* of the Lydian Pausanias.

He was greatly venerated in the cloister; often, at dusk, the monks gathered round him, and he read them, complaisantly, a few episodes of his Memoirs, depicting for them the insupportable glare of the sun in the Ethiopian lands, the strange mists of the northern seas, the warm mildness of the breeze of Hippalus, which leads to Taprobane, and the mysterious perfumes that float over the rivers of India when night falls. Then he narrated terrible or touching adventures, and above all told them the sacred legends that he had collected while wandering in Palestine, taking care mischievously to signal their contradictions, for his skepticism had increased with age.

That day, the day of the decapitation of the Precursor, after the evening meal, as they were sitting in the garden, a novice asked Hierocas whether he had ever heard anything concerning the life or death of the Baptist. Hierocas reflected for a moment, gazing into the distance at the sun descending into the sea, and then he invited the novice to sit beside him, and, the monks having drawn closer, craning their necks like avid children, he spoke.

What can I tell you about the person who is our protector? You know his life of a prophet, a life of mortifications and abstinences, the rigor of which he only interrupted to abuse is enemies, who were surely enemies of the true faith. As for his death, it is unforgettable, and the artist who copied the mosaic in our chapel has been able to embellish it further by the charm of his artistry. It is not, therefore about John that I would like to talk to you, but about the woman who was his executioner.

It is necessary not to think ill of Herodias,[1] and it is important to forget, in talking about her, the legitimate insults that saints and doctors have heaped upon her, for those saints and doctors were passionate men, and the very character of their passion prevented them from understanding the passions of others and from grasping the necessity of certain actions. Have you ever thought that it would have been frightful if the Baptist had not been put to death? It was evidently necessary that he be decapitated, and Herodias was the divine instrument.

Do not believe, however, in a special miracle; it was by natural ways that Herodias was led to act in the fashion that you know. She obeyed her virtues, her weaknesses and her energy; she was guided by her nature and her intelligence. This is what I have learned about her; you will forgive me if this story contradicts your belief in her regard and if the picture that I am going to give you of Herodias is not in accordance with the image of her that you have formed.

Herodias was a melancholy princess, and that melancholy even added to her beauty, a precious and rare beauty. The artist that I mentioned just now was able to

---

1 The name Herodias, attributed by many writers to Salome's mother and the wife of Herod, was attributed by Stéphane Mallarmé, in one of his most famous poems, to Salome herself; some of his acolytes followed his example.

render all the splendor of that virgin, and she has shown himself to his eyes as she was, charming and sad at the same time, with the morose smile at the corner of her lips of a child disappointed without ever having known anything. Imagine her thus, then, with her white tunic embroidered with scarlet flowers, her mantle of violet cloth and her golden tiara.

It was clad in that fashion that she had the custom of wandering in the gardens where she amused herself, especially in the evenings, when the brutal ardors of the sun ceased to violate the sadness of the olive-trees, penitent trees that seemed to be covered by an eternal ash. Herodias was meditative, but she only gave herself to dreams after having taken what was essential from reality. Her mind was subtle, alert and curious, and as she cherished solitude, she spent long hours meditating on what she had seen.

She would not have been a woman if matters of amour had not struck her first and foremost. As soon as she emerged from adolescence, it was the spectacle that lovers provide that surprised her eyes. She lived in a petty land where, although she was a princess, she could not ignore the existence of those who surrounded her. As her mother neglected her, she often went out with maidservants, and allowed herself to be guided by them, finding pleasure in seeing things for which she would have dared to search.

On the slopes of the dry and powerfully embalmed hills she often encountered couples who passed by intertwined. Thus, she soon knew what the joys of first love might be. She imagined them to be very noble and very beautiful, simple and refined, penetrating and good, gentle and poignant at the same time. She created for herself a marvelous realm over which her mind reigned, and was ambitious really to live in it.

After having seen tenderness united, however, she saw, on the same pathways, abandoned lovers and lovers fallen out of love. She understood by that the disillusionment of tenderness that pales and dies; she imagined the heartbreak that must follow the ruination of dreams.

It was to the lassitude of carnal possessions that her young mind attributed those disenchantments and distresses, and in order to keep intact the phantom of amour that she had created, she swore to remain chaste for the man she loved, and only to give her body to those from whom she would only be able to obtain vivid and temporary jubilations.

Doubtless she would have been a sad, delicate and voluptuous princess if she had not encountered the Precursor. She was in her mother's litter one day when the eater of locusts emerged on to the road and abused the queen. She did not hear the abominable insults, she only saw the prophet's face, his illuminated eyes, his aquiline nose, his russet and curly beard and his gestures of imprecation.

From that moment on she was able to comprehend that she had only ever imagined imperfectly the sentiments and sensations that amour engenders. She forgot her desires for sensuality and swore never to love anyone except the man who had been found on her route.

When Herod's soldiers had imprisoned the Baptist in the jails of Machaerus, Herodias was glad to be living near the man she cherished, but then desires assailed her, she thought about the joys of first possessions that embellished the face of lovers, she sensed her will weakening, she feared being one day similar to those who took pleasure in destroying, with their own hands, the happiness that the illusions of violent and virginal passions provides.

She did not think that the prophet might refuse the gift of that flesh, which she feared offering him, but the thought that one day he might reject her, thus overturning the palace of dreams and visions that her youth and adolescence had constructed, was odious to her, and she saw that death alone could deliver her from that danger.

As she was a woman, unconsciously egotistical, desirous of happiness and cruel, she did not think of dying, and when she had obtained Herod's oath, after she had danced before him, it was John's head that she demanded from the king: the head that, pale and cold, did not refuse her kiss when she took it from the hands of the executioner who had just been the protector of her dream and her amour.

"Perhaps that is the true story of Herodias," Hierocas concluded, "and it would not displease me to think so."

Illusion

THAT day, Cleomenes and Typhis were conversing in their villa in Syracuse with the Jew Theudas, a disciple of Plato, when they learned that the barbarian Odoacer, at the head of his Turcilingians, had just snatched the purple from the debilitated shoulders of Romulus Augustulus. They were greatly afflicted by it, not because they loved Rome and the phantom of imperium that was sinking thus into darkness, but they understood that with the ultimate heir of Caesar an entire world—theirs, the one they had cherished—was collapsing irrevocably.

Silently, Typhis and Cleomenes hid their faces and began to weep, while Theudas, who was thinking about the death of Jerusalem, felt his heart swell with emotion. For a long time they remained thus; when the crimson of the skies was shredded by the fingers of night they saw in it a symbol, that of the end of empires and gods; their minds then went back to the origins, and the two Greeks having decided to make a pilgrimage, Cleomenes said to Theudas: "We'll depart tomorrow for the island of Crete, in order to see again, one last time, the land that was the cradle of the gods."

"I'll go with you," said Theudas; and with that, they separated.

✳

The next day, they embarked, and after a few days of fortunate sailing, they trod the sacred soil.

For a month they traveled the island; they wandered over the beaches that had seen the whiteness of Aphrodite, they camped on the banks of the River Therenos, at the very place where Zeus and Hera had celebrated their wedding, and in the night, they thought that they could hear over the country the clamors of Pasiphae pursuing the bull.

Everything spoke to their heart and mind; here, the Titans dwelt; there, in the forests of Lethe, Harmonia forgot Kadmos; the forest of Platania sheltered Europa; the river of the Triton first reflected the face of Athene; the Dictean mountains retained Artemis the huntress; and one evening, stirred by a mystical emotion, Typhis and Cleomenes showed Theudas a valley where Demeter, in thrice-labored fallow ground, had united with Bakkhos.

Theudas made no reply, and Typhis asked him then: "Why have you accompanied us, Theudas? Your unbelieving soul cannot be moved by the memory of so much glory and so much misfortune; it cannot shiver in the breath of the divine that is scattered here, by the hills and the plains, by the woods and the meadows."

"Yes," added Cleomenes, "what desires can impel you in Crete?"

"Alas, my friends, I have come to reanimate my faith and my hope."

"But your God does not inhabit these places," said Typhis.

"I could tell you that he is everywhere," Theudas replied, "but that metaphysical response would not be sufficient for you. Know, however, that since the destruction of the walls of the immortal city, there are few countries where the one you call my God, and whom I would prefer to call *the* God, manifests his mysterious presence so forcefully. One might think that on this island, he guides and dominates those who believe in him, those who evoke him with a creative ardor. A spirit palpitates over these hills and these valleys, and for a moment I hoped to grasp it."

"Explain yourself, Theudas," said Cleomenes.

"Gladly, my friends. Listen, and you will perhaps see how dominating the illusion can be that engenders faith, and how, whether sublime or stupid—for you will judge in accordance with your intimate ideas—it is the master of human beings."

Nearly fifty years ago, a young Jewish shepherd named Moses lived in one of the grottoes of Mount Ida, whose bald head you can see from here. He lived soberly and simply, as his ancestors had lived in the plains of Judea, nourishing himself on medlars and arbutus-berries, olives that he pickled, sometimes honey, and, in winter, milk and chestnuts. All day long he grazed his flock on the grassy mountainside, and in the evening he often lay down in the midst of his ewes, in the woods of cypresses and maples.

Living alone, Moses was meditative, he knew how to retreat within himself, and he loved the dreams with which he amused himself. With regard to the destiny of his ancestors he was not unaware of anything. An old rabbi, doubtless an Essene, who had withdrawn into solitude, had educated him, and had left him when he died a few sacred scrolls, which were the shepherd's surest companions.

In the precious manuscripts he read ancient annals, and he was inflamed by the reading of great deeds accomplished. He incarnated by turns the heroes and the priests of Yahveh, and he thought about liberating his oppressed brethren, as Gideon and Jephthah had done.

The supreme misfortune of the people of Israel, his dead master had told him, was no longer seeing the waves of the benevolent Jordan or the walls of the divine city. Moses felt that he was in exile, and often, as he brought his lambs back at dusk, he wept for his destiny and that of the children of Juda. So, in leading his sheep over Ida, he did not seek to perceive, under the rocks, the caverns inhabited by the Dactyle ironsmiths and musicians; rather he expected the burning bush to appear one day to the dazzled eyes of the prophet.

One night, when he had meditated longer than usual, he heard a voice say to him: "Moses, I have chosen you to lead your brethren again to the Promised Land, from which their sins have expelled them, and to which expiation should recall them."

Moses did not hesitate. He thanked the Lord for having chosen him, and the next day, he quit his flock in order to be able to lead the people of God back to the cradle. In the cities and the countryside, he announced the good news, and the Jews gathered around him to listen. As he had other revelations he became more specific; Yahveh had promised him that before the year had elapsed, his children would see the lost fatherland again.

He now had an entire cortege. Poor Hebrews followed him, acclaiming and blessing him. Soon, the rich came with him; they quit their houses, sold their villas and their fields, forgot their counters and the gold that they had accumulated; they gave no more thought to the ships travelling the oceans for them; they abandoned their festival clothes, girded their loins with rope, armed their hands with a staff and prepared for the exodus.

One morning, Moses brought them all together. It was in the plain where we slept, which is crowned by white mountains, the plain populated by oleander and myrrh. They all came. Their leader revealed that he was the awaited Messiah, the predicted anointed, and gave them to understand that the following Sabbath was the day assigned for their deliverance.

They uttered clamors of delight, and Moses, having raised above the crowd the scrolls of the law, ordered them to follow him to the place that Yahveh had designated.

"As the slaves of Pharaoh passed over the Red Sea, as the sons of Nun passed over the Jordan, you will traverse the sea and you will reach the Promised Land."

Having said that, he put himself at their head; they traversed the whole island, only stopping to praise God, and on the eve of the Sabbath they arrived at the shore of the sea, where they camped on the sand near the promontory of Dion.

With their heads circled by sacred ribbons, they spent the night in prayer, lending an ear to the perfumed harmonies of the waves that still held scattered within them a little of the foam that had served as the cradle of the goddess. Moses separated himself from his people; he had climbed the rock that overlooked the waves, and there he waited, trying to penetrate the darkness, hoping for the promised miracle. When dawn came, his faithful followers came to stand at the extreme tip of the cape. They extended their arms toward him, and Moses' face was suddenly illuminated.

"Look!" he cried, and his hand indicated the far horizon. "There is the land flowing with milk and honey, and there is the plain that once cradled the city of palms. The orchards are quivering in the morning breeze, the vines sagging under the weight of grapes; I can see the child of Jephunneh and the waters are inclining before us."

The people threw themselves on to the strand. What Moses had said to them, they all saw, and, one among them having said that he perceived the hills of Sion, they rushed forward in tumult and went into the sea, which received them. Singing, they marched on, going until the waves had covered their heads, only falling silent when the bitter brine closed their mouths, and they descended into the abyss, believing that they were treading the soil of the fatherland.

From the summit of the promontory, Moses watched them, ecstatic. He saw them advance over the paths of the rendered Canaan, and when their arms rose up, still convulsive, over the foamy crests, it seemed to him that they were picking the marvelous fruits charging the illusory branches. Soon, the place was deserted; all of them, men and women, old people and children, had forsaken the isle of exile; and when the last one had disappeared, Moses, who could distinguish the floating cadavers in the distance, thanked God in a loud voice and, in his turn, he precipitated himself into the sea, which rose up to receive him.

✳

"Thus died Moses and the Jews of Crete," Theudas concluded.

"They died happy, for they believed, and their God loved them, since he gave them the living and blissful illusion," said Typhis.

"I envy them," said Cleomenes. "Like them, on a summer morning, I would like to contemplate Olympus; and—who knows?—perhaps one day I shall salute the returned immortals."

"And I," said Theudas, "would like to see Jerusalem triumphant, and doubtless I shall see it thus before dying, for nothing can take hope away from us, the tenacious Jews."

The Miracle

FOR long years, Hospitius, the confessor, embalmed the city of Nice with the perfume of his virtues. Hospitius lived in the distant time when Pépin, known as Héristal, led the descendants of Mérowig, as they guided the oxen drawing their carts,[1] but Hospitius paid little heed to that line of degenerate kings, whose authority, in any case, did not extend as far as those florid beaches. He was a poor God-fearing priest, animated by the flame that makes apostles and martyrs. Although he was a bishop, he had renounced the pomp of the episcopate. In his palace he lodged the sick, and he slept in a hut covered with thatch that he had built in the middle of the palatial courtyard.

When he was not in the city, which happened often, he visited the fishermen of the coast and, while soothing their woes, he tried to make them forget the worship of Poseidon and that of the marine nymphs. In his excursions, he was always accompanied by the discreet Fabius, his servant and friend, and in the evening,

---

1 The warrior Pépin d'Héristal (635-714) was the *de facto* ruler of the Frankish Kingdom, which he united by conquest, from 680 until his death.

when the two men found themselves alone on the fine gilded sands, the good bishop preached forbearance to the deacon, for Fabius was choleric and gladly struck with his closed fist the mariners who claimed to have gone astray in pursuit of the god Proteus.

When Hospitius was nearly a hundred years old he died in Nice, on his return from a journey. His priests exposed his body in the wretched cabin where the saintly bishop had died after having lived there. They had the doorway enlarged for that purpose, made a large breach in the facing wall, and for four days the people filed past the mortuary bed around which the most wretched of the paupers that Hospitius had the custom of nourishing were kneeling.

At the end of the bed, the faithful Fabius was seated and, between his pious hands, he supported the trans-figured head of the confessor, which faith had inflamed. Until the hour of the funeral, he refused to take any nourishment, preparing himself thus, as he had made a vow to do, to quit the world and bury himself in the monastery of the Isles[1] in order to merit there by his austerities a humble place at Hospitius' side in the celestial realm.

On the morning of the obsequies, Fabius, although weakened by his rude abstinence, was one of those who carried the saint's coffin. All the people accompanied their bishop, invading the church and its crypts, join-ing the clamor of their "Vae! Vae!" with the psalmodies of the monks and the liturgies of the priests. When

---

1 The reference is to the famous monastery founded by Saint Honoratus in the isles of Lérins in the fourth century.

Hospitius had been buried, Fabius put his hand against the sepulcher, took a little of the sacred dust, enveloped it in a coarse cloth and carried it away with him, for, in his monastic cell, he wanted to live with the memory of Hospitius and, at the same time, enable his ascetic brethren to benefit from the prerogatives that God would not fail to attach to the precious mud.

The next day, Fabius, after having spent the night in prayer again, enquired about a vessel departing for the Isles, but there was none in the port, for all of them intended to go to the Sicilian coast.

Desolate, Fabius was walking on the shore when he saw a ship preparing to set sail. On the strand, the mariners of the crew were loading jars of oil. Fabius approached them and enquired as to their destination. The oldest of the mariners ceded to his request.

"If our God, the God of Abraham, who commands the waves and the wind, wishes it, we shall set our course for Marseille," he said.

Fabius remained quite perplexed, for he had recognized thus that the people manning the galley were of the Jewish race. He did not trust the men of that nation and dared not make them the confidence of the deposit he was carrying, nor the place to which he wanted to go. He sat down on the sand, and meditated for a long time. Perhaps he had a celestial inspiration, for he stood up and, addressing himself again to the man who had replied to him, he asked him whether the vessel could take him to Marseille.

"Gladly," replied his interlocutor, "if you want to take your place alongside the rowers; we already have one passenger, a rhetor from Alexandria, a client of the idol Hermes, who is going to Nemausa."

Fabius accepted, and the same evening, abandoning the City of the Victory, the ship set forth. The sea was smooth and calm, so transparent that one could see the green tresses of the algae in the depths; a propitious wind inflated the sails, and, the oarsmen being vigorous and adroit, the prow cleaved the waves boldly.

Fabius suffered a great deal from the company in which he found himself. The Jews, although they had sacrificed the Lord, were joyful, and scarcely refrained from blasphemy. The deacon was very embarrassed by that, but out of regard for the consecrated ash, he remained quiet, fearing that if he admonished the impious individuals he might be abandoned on some rock. The society of the rhetor scarcely consoled him, and when he was sitting in the poop it was necessary to submit to the conversation of Cleon—that was the Graeculus' name—who related absurd fables about dolphins, an animated troop of which was following the vessel's wake.

With those torments, a greater preoccupation was mingled: how could he disembark at the convent? When that care assailed him, he reproached himself bitterly for lacking faith in God, and if he had not recognized that he was unworthy he would have walked over the waves to the monastery.

Soon, however, a perfumed wind ran over the waves and the Isles appeared on the horizon. The sailors bent over their oars because they wanted to give a wide berth to the orchards of the sea, but when they arrived within sight of the monastery an unknown power immobilized their oars, and in spite of the breeze inflating the sails, the ship stopped.

"Someone among us," said one of the oarsmen, "has doubtless blasphemed in name of the one God, and Adonai is punishing us by striking us with impotence, perhaps until the blasphemer is punished."

At those words, Cleon burst out laughing, so stupid did the superstitions of the Jews seem to him, and he said to Fabius: "Whatever is happening to us is to teach us not to be frightened, along with these men haunted by such stupid beliefs; assuredly it is some malicious Triton who, in order to mock these red-bearded barbarians, has seized our oars in his powerful hands."

But Fabius was not listening to Cleon. He threw himself to his knees on his bench, thanked Jesus for the help that he had just given him, and then, having risen to his feet, he told the Jews who he was, why he had lied to them, and explained the miracle of the immobile galley to them.

"Impious men," he cried to them, "if you are captive in the midst of the waves like this, it is because Jesus, our savior and our king, has wanted the memory of his son Hospitius to be perpetuated by me, Fabius, his very humble servant, in that holy monastery."

A few Jews, frightened and irritated by those words, wanted to fall upon Fabius; the old mariner, who was their chief, stopped them.

Without saying a word, he dived into the water, returned to the surface, climbed aboard the ship again, and lifted up the oars with a violent thrust. He showed the sailors that octopodes had enlaced the oars in their tentacles, linking them together, even fixing them to the keel, and thus hampering the vessel.

"Is that your God?" he asked Fabius, ironically. "Or yours?" he continued, addressing Cleon.

Cleon and Fabius remained silent. Cleon was vexed by the subtlety of the Jew and Fabius admired the infinite means by which the master of the world accomplished his designs.

In spite of that, the deicides did not want to keep Fabius aboard, for they feared his malefices. They turned aside from their route in order to take the deacon to the monastery. Fabius rendered thanks to Heaven, and when he set foot on land he turned to the old pilot and questioned him: "You don't want to incline before the son of God? You don't want to recognize that he alone sent the marine monsters to stop your course and favor my designs?"

The Hebrew shrugged his shoulders and replied: "I'd rather believe that they came of their own accord."

Cleon approved by nodding his head and smiling, while the deacon, clutching the relic to his chest, fled.

The Penitents

"IT was, in everyone's opinion," said Anselme, "a very morose salon, that of the Marquise de Grault, a lady canoness of I know not what chapter. Not that it was not frequented, but the habitués were severe and austere people, all priests or shriveled old scholars; a few Jansenists were even to be found there, and it was the last house in which theology and religious dogma were still debated. I was introduced to Madame de Grault's house by my uncle, a chartist of the old school, and I had ended up taking pleasure in that milieu, so different from those in which I usually moved. The men who came there were subtle, enlightened, erudite without pedantry, fertile in anecdotes and quips. I have retained a few of their stories, the ones that satisfied me most, and among them is the one I'm going to tell you.

"That evening, there had been talk of the people of Israel; the discussion had, in fact, been restrained from the religious viewpoint, and a bishop *in partibus* had said a few good things about the necessity of loving the Jews.

"'Are they not ready to become Christians?' he asked. 'We ought to believe it, and the highest dogmatic authorities have sustained the future recall of the Jews. Not to mention the Fathers of the Church, was it not our Bossuet who declared: *The Jews will come back one day, and they will return never to go astray again.*'

"'That's true,' someone replied, 'but orthodoxy scarcely anticipates the return of Israel to the Church until Judgment Day.

"'I don't think so,' replied the bishop—who was, I fear, a figurist. 'It's said expressly that the Church will suffer cruelly in giving birth to Benoni, and everyone knows that Benoni stands for Juda; so the Jews will return to the cradle before the end of the world. That, at any rate, was the opinion of the illustrious Duguet.'[1]

"'Those are noble thoughts,' replied an aged archeologist, who had kept silent thus far, 'but I don't have any confidence in the realization of your dream, Moneigneur.'

"'Why?' asked the bishop.

"'For the Jews to return to the altar, it would first be necessary for them to repent.'

"'That has happened to several of them,' affirmed a young abbé. 'Perhaps God can enlighten the others?'

"'Certainly,' said the archeologist. 'Nevertheless, I scarcely believe in the sincerity of Jewish remorse, that race being hardened and malicious.'

"'Have you special reasons for affirming that?' asked the bishop.

"'Permit me,' said the archeologist, 'to tell you a story that I recently read in an old manuscript.'

---

1 The reference is to Jacques-Joseph Duguet's *Explication du livre de la Genèse* (1732) and his fanciful decryption of chapter 35, in which Rachel's son "Benoni" (otherwise Benjamin) is born.

"'Gladly,' everyone exclaimed, and the archeologist, having demanded silence recounted."

❋

It was in the last months of the year 1492. In response to the prayers of the most holy Inquisition, King Ferdinand had expelled from his kingdom the sons of Abraham loyal to their faith, and along all the roads, to the north and the south, the east and west, going toward England and toward Africa, toward Portugal and toward Constantinople, one encountered the sad flock of exiles seeking the Promised Land again. Only a few families remained on Spanish soil, who had renounced their centuries-old error. Benevolently, the Church had opened its doors to the repentant sinners, extending its protection over them, but also its surveillance, for it feared that the new converts might return to their former idolatry, as dogs return to their vomit, and it recalled them to the good by means of torture and pyres.

One day, in Toledo, the Inquisitor received in audience a group of those Maranes, as they had called their fugitive brethren. A former rabbi, one celebrated for the ardor of his controversies, the depth of his exegesis and the extent of his science was conducting the neophytes. He spoke in the name of all of them, and he explained to the monk the desire by which they were moved. He claimed that their recent conversion, and even the purificatory water of baptism, were insufficient to redeem their past sins; the sacred water, in touching them, had certainly effaced the blackness of their souls, but it had not enabled them to expiate the crime of the ancestors that they had perpetuated by constantly denying the name of the true God.

The Inquisitor approved; he recommended to them, as efficacious means, severe fasts, flagellation and also the usage of cilices and hair shirts. But Rab Ascher—that was the orator's name—shook his head and declared that those means, although excellent, could not satisfy them. The worthy Dominican, only having at his disposal, by way of expiatory punishment, torture and the pyre, remained quite perplexed, and he begged Rab Ascher to explain.

Rab Ascher assented. He told the monk that his intention was to found a new order, that of Penitents, and to build a monastery into which he and his companions would withdraw in order to beg for pardon, day and night, for the abominable act committed by their forefathers, and to expiate it at every hour by prayer, abstinence and repentance.

The Inquisitor praised Rab Ascher and his friends highly for their good sentiments; he promised to support their request, and mediated so well in their favor that at the end of 1495, Rab Ascher was able to install the order of Penitents in a convent not far from Toledo.

For five years the piety of the Penitent friars won the admiration of Spain. People came from all directions to salute Rab Ascher and his flock, and great culpables, among those who crucified Christ daily, asked to pass through the doors of the monastery in order to redeem themselves. The rare few who were admitted to share the existence of the Penitents astonished the crowd by relating, on their return, the terrible exercises of piety to which the Maranes delivered themselves.

In the cloister, in an immense gallery, the scenes of the Passion were represented, and the individuals, of natural size and a gripping reality, frightened the mind and hallucinated the senses. The gallery was paved with sharp stones, between which iron spikes surged, barbed and chipped, and every day, the brothers traveled it, dragging themselves on their knees, tearing their flesh. They stopped before each tableau, striking the ground with their foreheads, and, bloodied, they deplored by turns each of the instruments of the divine torture; then, having reached the end of the frightful avenue, they stood up against the wall and, with their arms extended as if crucified, they cried out that they repented.

After five years, however, singular rumors began to run around the region. Vagabonds who spent the night near the monastery had heard strange chants; peasants out late had remarked that the cellars of the abbey were illuminated in the evening; others affirmed that they had seen Rab Ascher himself strolling in the abbatial gardens at dawn, his head circled by strange ribbons; a varlet reported that one Friday, having been able to approach a ventilation shaft, he had seen the brethren sitting in a small crypt around a candelabrum with seven branches and reading in large deployed scrolls.

All these stories reached the ears of a few familiars of the Inquisition; they made a report, and the Inquisitor, suspecting the Penitents of judaizing, resolved to wait for the eve of the Jewish Passover in order to surprise the monks. That was done, and the Inquisitor praised himself for his perspicacity, for on that eve of the commemoration of the Exodus, the monastery having been slyly invested, Rab Ascher and his community were surprised eating unleavened bread, the paschal lamb and bitter herbs, singing consecrated Hebrew hymns.

The Penitents did not put up any resistance; they allowed themselves to be bound and taken to the dungeons of the Holy Office. Their trial did not take long to prepare; the crime was patent and the punishment entirely indicated: the fire. So the chronicler would not have insisted on that banal story if he had not wanted to conserve for us the extraordinary responses of Rab Ascher. When the rabbi was summoned before the tribunal, he was asked to explain the singular rites that he had instituted, and the reason for the terrible austerities of which the scars on his face and his knees gave evidence.

"Were you repenting?" asked the Inquisitor.

"Certainly," replied Rab Ascher, "and I'm still repenting."

"What reason, then, drove you to return to your abjured religion?"

"You will understand when you understand the nature of my repentance."

"What was it?"

"This is it. I deplored the crown of thorns and the red cloak, because the crown and the cloak made a king out of the carpenter's son. I wept for the nails, the hammer, the spear and the sponge, and above all the wood of the cross, for the hammer and the nails, the sponge and the spear, and the wood above all, have made a god of the man of Nazareth. By incising my face, and carving my limbs, I was begging the pardon of the only God. Almighty Jehovah, for the crime of my unconscious brethren."

"A crime? You're contradicting yourself, rabbi."

"No!" cried Rab Ascher. "Is it not a crime to set up another divinity in the face of the Unique? Is not that sin the most abominable that my ancestors had committed? For centuries, they have borne the weight of the sin, and the man of your race that you adore has been cruel to them; but they do not understand the significance of the persecutions they suffer, the martyrdom to which they are subject, and their suffering is valueless because it does not have their consent. And it is for that reason that my companions and I assumed the weight of the deplorable action and we have subjected ourselves to the conscious repentance that cleanses and redeems."

No one responded to Rab Ascher. Horror, affirms the author of the chronicle, closed the mouths of the judges, as it stopped his words.

"And from all that," the archeologist added, "I have concluded the vanity of the remorse of the Jews."

"I cannot help finding that conclusion a trifle hasty," said Anselme. "To begin with, I believe that few Israelites, especially of our time, would be capable of comprehending the singular folly of that Rab Ascher, who, by virtue of the religious perversity of his imagination, surely merited being a Christian. Then again, the case of age-old remorse can rarely echo among the descendants of Caiaphas, and if I were of the lineage of

Jacob I would have difficulty in tormenting my conscience and delivering it to the rack of repentance under the pretext that a petty Roman procurator ordered the crucifixion, in accordance with the abominable custom of his era, of a poor Hebrew who was nourished on prophets, psalmists and the marrow of the Talmud, and was preaching the doctrines of the rabbi Hillel through the taverns of the popular quarters."

"Did you say all that to Madame de Grault?" asked Nalle.

"Alas, yes, and that house was closed to me, because I declared that I regretted the martyrdom of Jesus as much as that of Giordano Bruno, that their deaths moved me equally. But to return to my Jews, I declare that if I found even one capable of tormenting his mind and yielding to despair because of what is commonly called, without reason, the crime of Israel, I would doubt his reason far more than his sincerity."

The Confession of Don Juan

"YES," Anselme admitted, "It's a strange story, and I'm astonished that no traveler has reported it; but I've searched for it in vain in the most forgotten collections and the best-known narratives, and you're doubtless unaware of it. So, I'll narrate it to you, and at the same time, I'll tell you the circumstances in which it was told to me."

It was about twenty years ago. I had just completed my studies, and I completed them by traveling. After having visited Italy and Sicily, I embarked for Greece and I began my pilgrimage over the soil of Hellas with the very soul of the young Anarcharsis,[1] which I have since lost. I stayed for a few months in Athens, and then, with a friend who was able to read Homer to me, we departed for the hollow valley in which great Lacedaemon once stood, for we wanted to wander on

---

1 As in *Voyage du jeune Anarcharsis en Grèce* (1787) by Jean-Jacques Barthélemy.

the banks of the Eurotas of the green reeds, evoking the memory of the swan and that of the divine virgin.

One evening, as we were approaching Magula, the poor village that stands in the same place where the terrible Sparta once was, we stopped near a white house adjacent to a chapel built on the side of the road. On the threshold we were greeted by a hermit with a venerable air, attracted by the sound of our footsteps, who offered us hospitality. We accepted, and when we had taken a very simple meal we questioned our host.

He told us that he had been living for some year in that plain, dominated by the Taygete, and, occupying that isolated dwelling alone, he guarded a venerated tomb located in the crypt of the chapel, to which he would take us if we wished. On our affirmative response, the hermit lit a resin torch and we followed him.

We went into the little church and then, our guide having opened a door behind the altar, we descended after him in a steep and cold stairway that ended in the grotto. The grotto was quite broad, but rather low; the walls and the columns had been coated with a bright stucco that sparkled in the light of several lamps suspended from the ceiling. In the middle stood the sepulcher, entirely made of blue marble, monumental and superb.

It was composed of a rectangular sarcophagus, on the lid of which was sculpted an old man with a long beard, whose head was supported by a woman leaning over the side of the tomb. The face of the old man was calm and peaceful, and his empty eyes seemed to be contemplating the person leaning over him with bewilderment. The face of that guardian was veiled, but beneath the veil one divined a strange, sovereign and mysterious beauty; one sensed that the unknown artist whose chisel had caused the unknown woman to live again had not dared show to humans the divine splendor that had been revealed to him.

No name was inscribed on the marble of the sarcophagus, but only a verse from Euripides that my companion read: *Many souls have succumbed for me on the banks of the Scamander.* We looked at one another, and doubtless the hermit surprised an anxious curiosity in our gaze, for he raised his torch and extended a finger toward the old man, and simply pronounced two words, which left us dazed with astonishment: "Don Juan."

Then, as we remained mute and immobile, he lowered his torch, sat down on a stool at the foot of the sepulcher, and spoke.

A long time ago—months, years, centuries—a convent of monks occupied part of this pain. It was placed under the invocation of the holy Queen Helen,[1] and a fragment of the true cross was venerated there. The abbot of the monastery was Hilarion, a pious man, savant and charitable, whose virtues were renowned.

1 The saint known in English as Saint Helena is known in France as Sainte Hélène, thus facilitating the ironic mistake featured in the story. The sanctified Helen/Helena (c250-c330), born in Greece, was the consort of the Roman Emperor Constantius Chlorus and the mother of his successor, Constantine the Great; she is given much of the credit for orientating Constantine, and thus the Empire, toward Christianity.

This is what the chronicles say about Hilarion. He had the custom of wandering in the hills and the valley in order to collect wild herbs; often, he remained absent for days or weeks, leaving his flock without a pastor, and it was said that he was favored with visions and revelation.

One night, a clear and moonlit night, as Hilarion was coming back to the monastery, he had a singular encounter. He was walking at a rapid pace, hastening in order to be able to participate in the nocturnal office, when, at the corner of the road that led to the cloister, he perceived a man lying on the ground, clad in the brown robe of a pilgrim and also clutching a pilgrim's staff.

Hilarion drew closer and, as the moonlight was shining full in the face of the supine man he saw that he was an old man with a thick white beard. He thought that he was dead, and bent over him, but when he brushed his forehead with his hand the old man sat up abruptly, and said to Hilarion: "What do you want with me?"

"To help you," Hilarion replied, "and to take you to the monastery whose porch you can see over there. You'll find consolation there, peace, and, if you desire it, forgetfulness."

"Let me die where I am, I beg you," said the old man. "Don't remove me from this soil, which I love, to enchain me far from my happiness and my dream under those vaults, which I can see in advance and which I don't want to know. Leave me alone. I've come from the Occident and I want to die here."

"It shall be done in accordance with your desire," Hilarion replied. "Doubtless you have made a vow, and it is good that no one opposes it. But since you are approaching death, tell me who you are, and what your sins were."

"Who am I?" said the old man, with a start of pride and alarm. "Renown has certainly brought you my name one day, but I want even so to tell you again, begging you not to be frightened by it. My name is Don Juan."

"I know you, my son," said Hilarion, simply, "and I await your confession."

"What confession can I make to you, monk? Since you know me, you know my life, and I would not be telling you anything by relating my adventures to you, neither those that I have cherished and renounced, nor those of which I have despaired."

"You could tell me whether you repent," objected Hilarion.

"I have no repentance, only regrets, and soon I shall no longer have those, for I'm about to reach the very dear objective that is mine."

"What objective?"

"What objective, you say? I can see that it's necessary to tell you everything; perhaps then you'll let me die in peace. Listen to me, then. You might have believed, as everyone has believed, that debauchery alone was my guide and that my masters were my passions and my senses. Nothing of the sort, for I am the lover of the eternal dream and the immortal idea.

"It was in the spring of my life when the dawn illuminated my days that I had the blessed vision, the dominating vision that has brought me here in order to die. One morning, near my father's house, in the orchard of orange trees, under the trees illuminated by golden apples, I saw a woman coming toward me, naked, divine and simultaneously imperious and tender.

"Her memory still lives in my mind, her image fills my eyes and my heart, and she will embalm my body eternally. She had the movement of a swan, the arrogant grace of reeds, and her white arms were like silvery streams. She approached, gliding over the ground, placed her flowery fingers on my forehead and said to me, softly: 'Juan, I am Helen, look at me carefully, and now, go seek me throughout the world beneath the veil in which, for you, I shall dissimulate myself.'

"I sensed the caress of her lips, I fainted, and when my eyes opened again, she had disappeared.

"Since that day, monk, in all maidens and all women, I have pursued the lost Helen, the Helen who is scattered in all of them, but whom none can incarnate. I have tried to make the immortal live, and have never been able to do it, for the most beautiful, the most seductive, those who merit the admiration of men, only have one particle of the beauty of Helen. The divine inspiratrix lives in them, however, she animates them, she ornaments their bodies, she decorates their souls, and it is still her that one adores in the imperfect images in which a little of her splendor palpitates.

"I have known them all, and I have cherished all of them; they attracted me and captivated me by what they had retained of their creatrice, the immortal who is the matrix of beauty, but they soon wearied me, for they could not satisfy the plenitude of my desires, my dreams and my ambitions. Before recognizing that the living Helen cannot be resuscitated, I vagabonded through the world like the Wandering Jew; I experienced all amours, the basest and the most sublime, and found them all equal.

"Then, one day, harassed by fatigue, disappointed and saddened, my body withered and my soul aged, I renounced the struggle. I understood that my quest would always be vain, and that I would only find the one that I had glimpsed, the immutable beauty, beyond life.

"Then my feet, which had trailed so much mud after them, had the desire to tread the soil that her feet had brushed, my eyes desired to know the blessed earth where she had once had her transitory dwelling, and which her memory must have embalmed forever. I wanted to come to the place where she was born, and which keeps alive her memory and her image, in order that the murmur of the Eurotas, which had seen the eternal lover, would send me to sleep the good slumber, and that my eyelids would close under the sky that saw hers open, in an unforgettable morning."

As he said those words, Don Juan's head inclined on the abbot's shoulder, and quietly, he died.

Hilarion loaded him on to his back, and carried him to the convent like that. There, he was buried piously, because of his devotion to Saint Helen, and some time afterwards, an artist who was passing that way, and to whom the story was told, built Don Juan this mausoleum, on which he inscribed the words that you have just read, whose meaning escapes me:

Many souls have succumbed for me on the banks of the Scamander.

Until Death

THERE are tragic jealousies that are not common-place, jealousies that cannot lend themselves to the ridicule that it is conventional to cast upon the jealous. There are jealousies that are not external to amour but which, on the contrary, manifest it in a more profound, more decisive fashion, jealousies that emerge from the very wellsprings of passion, which are its seal, its proof, its bloody and redoubtably beautiful flower.

Those kinds of jealousies only reveal their existence in exceptional cases; they burst forth abruptly, in response to unexpected nervous shocks, in extraordinary circumstances; they are affirmed in accomplishing their work, and are extinguished after having struck. There are few examples of them and they are precious to collect. That is why the story of the Florentine Arrigi is seductive. I sometimes like to retell it, as it was told to me, one evening in August when the waves of the Rhône were undulating more voluptuously than usual.

At the end of the last century or the beginning of this one—no one has been able to tell me the exact date—an adventurous merchant named Léone was living in Arles. For part of the year he trafficked in Marseille, and often traveled, but always returned to Arles to forget the cares of business and savor the joys of amour.

Léone was, in fact, married. He had married a simple peasant woman, the most beautiful daughter of that region, in which all the maidens have the airs of Aphrodite, and he loved her passionately, having taken her for her beauty, the only fortune of which she disposed.

Dame Mion—that was the name of Léone's wife—cherished her husband, but she had not chosen him. They lived very happily, however: a facile and opulent life, surrounded by numerous friends which they liked to welcome to their home. Among the most assiduous guests was a gentleman from Florence, Sano Arrigi. He was a tender and melancholy young man who had arrived in Arles a few years before and had not left again, seduced by the mystery and splendor of the incomparable city where the sun adorns the ruins of marvelous flowers.

Sano was a fine talker; he knew touching and heroic tales, but above all he could talk about the Alyscamps, the cloisters, and the circle of ingenious things in which his taste for the past was exhibited. Léone had taken him in affection, and a few mutual services rendered had changed that affection into amity. As for Dame Mion, she could only smile when Sano was nearby.

One morning, Léone came to knock on Arrigi's door. He went in and informed his friend of his imminent departure. His business affairs were compromised; only a voyage to the Levant would permit him to reestablish them, and, as he did not want to take his wife into those distant regions, he was leaving her in Arles, and begged him to accept to look after her. Loyally, Sano consented.

After touching adieux, Léone embarked at Marseille, and his wife and Sano, who had accompanied him there, returned to Arles. There, Mion lived in reclusion; she only saw Arrigi, who came every day to inform himself regarding her desires and to take the evening meal with her, in order to distract her solitude.

During the hours that they spent together, Sano strove to tell Mion tender and diverting stories, but he often stopped, and they both remained silent, while she closed her eyes meekly.

One evening, six months after Léone had departed, as they were both in the arbor, Mion leaned toward Sano and asked him, in a very soft and emotional voice: "Sano, why don't you tell me that you love me?"

Sano started trembling in every limb. He looked into Mion's eyes, and he suddenly forgot his friend, who had departed confident in his promises. He felt passing through him the breath of amour that is even stronger than the breath of death. He leaned over, applied his lips to Mion's mouth, and said: "I've always loved you."

From then on, they lived happily. They felt that they had always been destined for one another, and that their bodies and souls were summoned to one another for all eternity, for they were religious and they believed in predestination. They loved one another without hiding, their amour being one of those that cannot stoop to pretence. They were unable to dissimulate the joy that they had in being lover and mistress, and were sometimes seen kissing in public. They had forgotten Léone's existence; they never thought about him, and never worried about knowing what had become of him.

Their happiness lasted two years, during which their tenderness increased in being satisfied. Their caresses had never had more charm for them, they had never felt more closely bound together; they were but one flesh and one mind, and they lived their lives reciprocally.

At the beginning of the third year, one afternoon in January, Dame Mion was informed by letter that her husband would arrive the following day. Neither she nor Sano became anxious, any more than if the return of a friend had been announced to them. They received Léone with joy, heaped him with caresses, and all three of them spent the day chatting joyously.

After the evening meal, Léone got up, embraced Sano, and told his wife that he would be delighted, after such a long time, to go into the conjugal bedroom. At those words, the two lovers seemed to emerge from a dream; they looked at one another in distress, and Sano abruptly seized his sword and struck Léone, who fell, appealing to his wife for aid; but the latter seized the weapon in her turn and killed him.

The servants shouted for help, people came, and Mion and Sano were seized. They put up no resistance and allowed themselves to be taken away, albeit after having escaped the arms holding them long enough to exchange an ardent kiss.

Judgment was passed on them. They did not defend themselves, not even deigning to respond to the questions that were put to them, and they remained motionless for the duration of the trial, looking at one another. They were condemned to have their heads cut off, on the same scaffold, on the same day.

They seemed satisfied, and when they were asked whether they had any protest to make, they extended their hands toward one another and said: "I love you!"

No jailers ever had any prisoners as docile as those two lovers; they were only suffering from being separated. When the day of the execution arrived they were joyful at the idea of seeing one another again, and they allowed themselves to be dressed without proffering a word and without resisting the executioner.

They encountered one another in the narrow corridor of the prison; they were allowed to approach one another, so great was the pity and admiration that their passion and their courage inspired. They hugged one another for a long moment, and then, in a few words, testified to the constancy of their tenderness and encouraged one another mutually to die well.

However, when they were in the square where the scaffold was set up, Sano showed an extreme emotion on learning that they wanted to strike him first, and he threw himself at the feet of the priest and the magistrates who were accompanying him, asking to see his mistress perish first.

His request was not granted immediately, but he entered into such a terrible fury then, and put up such resistance, that in order to avoid a supreme scandal, they acceded to his desire.

He calmed down as soon as he had seen Mion march to death, and his eyes shone with an incredible joy when he saw the head of his beloved fall. He was getting ready to go toward the scaffold boldly when the judge asked him why he had wanted to die last, suggesting that it was doubtless because he wanted to spare his lover the frightful spectacle of his execution.

Sano shook his head, and replied: "I wanted the blade to give me its last kiss."

The priest reprimanded him gently, for he saw him perishing in his sin, but Sano paid no heed to him, and, in a bitter voice, revealed the secret of his tormented heart.

"I also wanted to see her die first," he said, "because with me dead, a miracle might have been able to save her, and it was impossible for me to support the idea that she would live without me, especially if someone else were able to possess her."

The Supreme Kiss

SUCH as I found it in an ancient Italian chronicle, I will tell you the story of Léonora Barberi. It is the story of a passionate and energetic woman in love, who was able to give herself entirely to her passion and extract from it the sweetest and the most voluptuous as well as the most terrible emotions. She did not compose herself with her amour; she did not know the art of equilibrating her life, and preferred the disorder of action, even brutal and criminal, to the order of hypocritical existence. She was a beast of amour, and she followed the unique law that wild beasts follow in the forests and the mountains: the law of the satisfaction of needs. If she was refined, it was because she lived in a time when, above primitive barbarity, the formation was commencing of more delicate instincts; her savagery was therefore clad in complex sentiments; it was ornamented and embellished.

Léonora was born in Rome under the pontificate of Alexander VI. Her father, Galeno, was a much-prized armorer, and he was known to be protected by Cesare Borgia, who often had recourse to his services. Galeno's enemies even accused him of having sold to the enemies of the terrible Duce coats of mail that were defective, and at the very moment when they feared assassination. Misfortune had, indeed, determined that those men were stabbed, in spite of their protective coats.

Galeno's wife having died shortly after his daughter's birth, Léonora grew up in the armorer's shop, and she learned the tragedy of life in the stories of cavaliers who related their exploits while examining the blades of daggers and the points of rapiers. She gained virtues from that special education that were not customarily those of her sex, and she acquired a ferocious conception of the world; it appeared to her as an arena in which, by means of force and auxiliary cunning, robust animals fought, who always ceded to their passions and only experienced displeasure in not satisfying them.

Because she became very beautiful as she advanced in age she found herself surrounded and courted by all the young cavaliers of Rome. She resisted all solicitations, stood up to all assaults, and one day, she told her disappointed adorers that she was marrying Signor Barberi.

Luigi Barberi was an opulent gentleman of great nobility, but he was sixty years old and his fiancée was sixteen. Léonora's courtiers, in order to calm their chagrin, declared that the armorer's daughter was less ardent than ambitious; more than one, however, hoped that he would obtain from the wife what the virgin had refused.

Their hope was disappointed. Old Barberi took his wife to a villa he possessed in the middle of the Sacco valley, near the fiefs of Colonna, and for five years, Léonora remained far from Rome. When she came back to install herself in the Palazzo Barberi, she brought with her a ten-year-old child, to whom she testified a maternal affection. She called him Tiberto. To those who asked who the child was, she related that, on the very night of her wedding, she had found him on the threshold of her dwelling and that, out of respect for the fortune that had taken her there, she had resolved to keep him with her and raise him.

Léonora adored Tiberto. As Galeno was dead and she had never experienced tenderness for Barberi, she gave the child all the treasures of an enveloping and warm affection. She watched him grow up as one sees a beautiful flower that one has cared for slowly blossom, and as he grew older her love was transformed.

At first she had cherished Tiberto as her son; when he was fifteen and she was twenty-six, she loved him more fraternally; she was the confidant of his juvenile aspirations and his first vague desires. For Tiberto she was the idol; he had never been able to consider her as a mother; she was a divine image of beauty placed beside him, and on which he modeled his dreams. In Léonora, he incarnated those dreams; she was the inspiration of the disturbances of adolescence; thanks to her he did not know the anguish of those who summon a distant and muted initiatrix. The day when he knew what it was to love, he loved Léonora, and Léonora loved him.

She loved him with all her contained ardor of an amorous woman; she gave him all that her chaste youth and her morose wifely maturity had accumulated of passionate softness, tender violence and terrible voluptuousness. She was truly born on the evening when

Tiberto kissed her. One might have thought that her true nature had only been revealed at that moment, and, at the same time as her powerful love for Tiberto, a terrible hatred blossomed in her soul against her husband.

When she emerged from the arms of her lover, the sight of the old man was odious to her, and she rendered him responsible for the remorse that Tiberto sometimes felt when he thought about the old man's benefits. The presence of her husband reminded Léonora constantly that she had not reserved the flower of her flesh for the man she loved, as she had kept the blossoming of her heart for him, and she hated Barberi all the more as her regrets grew with her satisfied passion. She trembled with anger in thinking that the old fool might grow older still, persistently, and constrain her to conceal an amour that could only be fully satisfied on the day when she could proclaim it to everyone.

One morning, at first light, she went into her husband's room and stabbed him; she had been unable to resist any longer the desire for murder that had seized her. She had not had the hypocritical prudence to hire an assassin, and when people came to tell her that Barberi had been found inanimate and bloody, she did not consent to play the comedy of amazement. Thus, she was vehemently suspected, and, on the denunciation of a valet who affirmed that he had seen her entering her husband's room at dawn, the Pope—it was Clement VII—ordered that she be delivered to justice.

She allowed herself to be seized and did not deny any of the accusations, not even denying the testimony of the valet. She was thought to be doomed, for the

Pope had declared that he would be inflexible for adultery, but on the day of the judgment, Tiberto presented himself before the tribunal and swore on the host that it was him who had assassinated Barberi out of jealousy. The testimony of the accuser was opposed to him; he replied that the night-shirt by which he was enveloped when he had committed the crime had misled the witness.

After having denied violently that Tiberto was the assassin, Léonora fell silent when the latter opposed to her denials a new and terrible oath. Tiberto was condemned to have his head cut off, and when Léonora withdrew, it was in the midst of the murmurs of pity and admiration of the crowd, who attributed to her the desire to preserve, at the price of her own life, the person she loved as a son.

In order to save Tiberto from death, Léonora attempted everything, for it was in that hope that she had accepted the lie that rendered her liberty. She had thought that she would be able to snatch Tiberto from the hands of the executioner and could flee with him to the desired happiness. It was all in vain. She ran into the inflexibility of the Pope and the rigor of jailers that she could not corrupt. On the eve of the day when Tiberto was to perish it was learned that Léonora, in despair, had quit the Palazzo Barberi.

The next day, in the midst of a crowd delirious with ferocious curiosity, Tiberto mounted the steps of the scaffold without disturbance or pallor. He looked around, seeking in the packed crowd for the woman he would have liked to have near him at that supreme moment. He saw nothing, and a terrible dolor contacted his face when the executioner seized him and made him kneel down. He did not budge, however, and waited; but the breathless people were then witness to a strange spectacle.

The executioner suddenly staggered, as if stunned, and the sword of justice escaped his hands. Then, the person who was serving as his aide, and whom no one had yet seen, seized the naked blade rapidly and struck Tiberto with a terrible blow. Then, throwing the abominable weapon away, she seized the young head that had just fallen and kissed it passionately, while the crowd cried out in horror on recognizing Léonora.

Without listening to the clamors, however, she addressed them all, and said to them: "It is from me that he received his only kisses; it is my arms that taught him voluptuousness; it is because of me that he lived; it is because of me that he had to die, and I could not have supported it if any hand but mine had delivered the final blow; it is me who had to have his supreme kiss of death, and I have had it, for his lips returned the kiss that mine gave him."

Having said that, she hugged the dear head one final time, and, holding it against her heart, she struck herself in her turn.

Honor

THERE is general agreement as to the fact that it is almost impossible to give a precise and exact definition to a word evoking a sentiment or a group of sentiments. What definition, for example, can be given to the word "amour," since that passion is manifest in a thousand different ways, to such a degree that in certain cases it presents itself under the appearance of hatred? But if there are various fashions of understanding amour, or jealousy, or even envy, there is usually sufficient agreement to determine general characteristics. It is not the same with regard to honor. That is because honor is generally a system of prejudices and conventions rather than an ensemble of sentiments. It is a word that is pronounced as confidently and as willingly, with as much emphasis and assurance, and as if everyone knew perfectly well what the term implies and the obligations that it represents. I do not know, however, any word whose conception is vaguer, and there are, to tell the truth, as many species of honor as there are of human beings.

But it is the manner in which women comprehend their honor, above all, that is troubling and disconcerting, being so multiple, contradictory and incoherent. One could compile a book of curious anecdotes on that subject, a book that would show the vanity of that social superstition. In that book I would willingly feature the story of the Marquise de Langallery.

※

Madame de Langallery, who was a former Mademoiselle de Nesmond and the sister of the Bishop of Montauban, had married one of the richest gentlemen of the Angoumois. She had married very young and had had a son, who was brought up by his uncle, the Bishop and was destined to enter holy orders.

Monsieur de Langallery loved ostentation, and took pleasure in entertaining; his dwelling was hospitable to the entire nobility of the Angoumois and the Périgord. The table was kept open there all the year round, and the fare was exquisite, in a region where it is commonly excellent.

If Monsieur de Langallery was considered one of the most gallant men in the province, the Marquise was regarded as one of the loveliest women. She was thirty-four years old and was in the flower of her sovereign beauty. She was reputed to have a great deal of intelligence, an intelligence without affectation, which came from natural gifts and not from assiduous cultivation, for she had no education and maintained an ardor, an energy and a violence that were entirely primitive, as we shall see in due course.

She was faithful to her husband, and also loved him very much; she had more than esteem for him, and would not have wanted to render him ridiculous in any fashion—which, in the Angoumois, at that time, was still the lot of deceived husbands; things have changed since. In spite of her fidelity, however, Madame de Langallery was nonetheless a gallant woman; by that I mean that she did not detest flattery, nor amorous speeches, when she knew that they were piquant without offending decency. In brief, she was adroit in conciliating her conjugal duties with those imposed by her beauty.

In the year that her son attained the age of eighteen, Monsieur de Langalerry summoned him to the château and held great celebrations for the occasion. Among the numerous society that had rendered to the Marquis' invitation was Monsieur de Bièvre, one of the most courteous and perfect cavaliers of the neighborhood. For a long time Monsieur de Bièvre had been court-ing Madame de Langallery. The latter had welcomed his homages and showed him a benevolent favor; she savored his speeches, which were exceedingly delicate and witty; she did her best to respond in kind, and did not dissimulate the satisfaction she had in being in his company.

She had admitted him into her most complete in-timacy, making him her counselor in matters of taste and pleasure, and listened to him with complaisance. Monsieur de Bièvre, whose temperament was ef-fervescent and lively, did not hide from Madame de Langallery that, if he amused himself with gallantries and bagatelles, in which he took pleasure, he retained the hope of being admitted one day to prove his at-tachment even more. To those advances, Madame de

Langallery had always responded in an ambiguous fashion that permitted her, in her own estimation, to remain morally faithful to her spouse, while not discouraging her servant.

Such a game, however, is not as honest as one pretends, and profligacy of the spirit and the sentiments prepares the body to fail. Without granting anything to Monsieur de Bièvre, Madame de Langallery came to promise him a great deal. How did she accord those promises with the fidelity that she had always maintained? Women have a thousand means of entertaining contradictory things in comfort. At any rate, Monsieur de Bièvre was put in the situation of no longer praying but requesting, and the likelihood of success, as soon as he thought the opportunity presented itself.

That opportunity was given to him by a hunting party. He departed one morning with the whole company in order to flush out a wild boar that had been spotted in a nearby wood. At the height of the game, however, when the beast had just quit its lair, he abandoned the post assigned to him, furtively, and returned to the château by a roundabout route, without being seen.

Very quietly, in order not to alert the few domestics who remaining in the house, he went up to the apartment nearest to Madame de Langallery's, and remained there, listening to see whether she was alone.

Immediately, he heard her order her chambermaid to go to fetch a basket full of figs from a distant vineyard. When he had seen the maid go out, he slipped into the room adroitly. He found Madame de Langallery in a state of virtual undress, unveiling charms that were not made to calm his passion. He put himself on his knees and did so with temerity, thinking thus to profit from her surprise and the good intentions that he believed her to have in his regard.

In that, however, he was much mistaken, for Madame de Langallery, who was quite astonished to see him there when she knew that he was at the hunt, resumed her intelligence and rejected him violently. With the most vivid irritation she criticized his conduct, asking him whether he took her for a wayward woman, and, blushing with shame, enveloped herself in a piece of cloth that came to hand.

At first, Monsieur de Bièvre replied to her very mildly, assuring her of his respect, and also exposing the violence of an amour that she had been able to encourage, but the Marquise was not appeased. She replied that she desired nothing as much as to punish his impudence, and added that if she had her domestics she would order them to give him a good hiding and throw him out of the window.

Then Monsieur de Bièvre lost all restraint; he reproached her for her bad faith, and, allowing himself to be drawn beyond the respect that he owed to a lady, he accused her of not having been miserly with her favors toward others who were perhaps baser, and even of lower status. So saying, he left abruptly, leaving Madame de Langallery in a terrible irritation.

Agitated by wrath, she went to the room where her son, who had not accompanied her husband, was in bed, suffering from a slight indisposition. She told him everything, shedding a torrent of tears, in despair that the young man, who was destined for the Church, was not in a position to avenge the insult that had just been offered to her.

Her discourse was so passionate and so furious, she was so beautiful and so touching in her anger, that she inflamed the young deacon's soul. He got up violently, pushed away his mother, who affected to want to retain him, seized a pistol that was hanging on the wall above his bed, went downstairs precipitately and set out in search of Monsieur de Bièvre. He encountered him as he was preparing to mount a horse in order to quit the château, marched toward him and, as Monsieur de Bièvre came to meet him, fired his pistol full into his chest and laid him dead on the pavement.

Madame de Langallery had followed her son. When she saw how he had avenged her on her insulter, she burst into transports of joy, took him in her arms and thanked him for having redressed the wrong that had been done to her. But her vengeance was doubtless not yet satisfied, for, letting go of her son, she approached Monsieur de Bièvre's cadaver and, snatching his own sword, she plunged it into the body several times, insulting him atrociously, like a Fury, shouting in a loud voice that she was redeeming her honor.

Thus, for that lady, it was honorable to entice a man by her attitudes, her soft expressions, her tender and engaging words; it was honorable to make him promises that she probably had no intention of keeping; honor consisted precisely in lacking loyalty to those promises, and a woman could emerge from her sex to the point that I have just described in order to escape the dishonor of having been seen almost naked by an amorous gentleman, to whom she had abandoned her hand while refusing to let him take her arm.

"You see, Nalle, how uncertain Madame de Langallery's doctrines were. You would, however, be wrong to despise her, for ours are, in that matter, not much more reliable, unless one puts honor, as I should like to do, in the exercise of virtue."

"It remains for us to agree upon virtue."

"My dear Nalle, I will call virtue, if you wish, the science that permit us to bring into harmony the respect that we ought to have for ourselves with the love that it is important to experience for others, and to conciliate the independence that is necessary to us with the liberty of our neighbor. The man who equilibrates in his being and in his life his duties toward himself and his duties to his neighbors, in accordance with the formulae of the old morality, is a virtuous man—and, let us say, an honorable man, since we started from honor."

The Glimpse

"NO," said Anselme, "I don't believe in the persistence of the personality. I don't know what the transformations are to which our self is subjected after death, but how do you think it can remain identical to itself when the cells of which it was the resultant are dissociated?"

"But if it doesn't remain identical to itself," replied Nalle, "it won't be the same."

"That's exactly what I meant," said Anselme, "and the transformations of our soul commence with the annihilation of the self that is so dear to us."

"You're not a believer, Anselme," said Claude.

"That's true," Anselme retorted, "if by that you mean that I don't attach myself to any religion, that I reject all confessional dogmas and that I'm even unaware of the horror of deism—but I claim that in that matter, the believers have no advantage over me."

"What do you mean?" asked Nalle.

"This: religious and pious people retain within them, somnolent and hereditary, that faith in the survival and immortality of the soul; it sleeps in a crease of their brain in which atavism is encrusted, and in certain difficult circumstances they awaken it, and it becomes for them a palliative that anesthetizes normal chagrins, often nourishing a hope that duty, if not tenderness, commands. But if, in the life of one of these traditionalists, one of those terrible dolors arrives that disturbs the equilibrium of human nature, you will see their faint hope carried away and broken by the tempest. What they have become habituated in the course of their existence to consider as the supreme buoy is the first to disappear, engulfed by the storm of their despair. And since we have adopted the custom of clarifying our ideological assertions with carefully chosen examples, let me support what I say with a true story."

Toward the end of the seventeenth century, a woman lived in Montpellier who had some celebrity in that city. She was married to a well-known magistrate, and her name was Madame de Lomelas. She had a great and justified reputation for intelligence; she was extremely open-minded; she was erudite but was able not to be pedantic; her judgment was sure and her taste perfect. Her home, where her conversation full of charm and wit had attracted the elite of society, was much frequented. Verses were read there, piquant, if not malign, epigrams were sharpened there; there was passionate discussion regarding the genius of Corneille and that of Racine; *Oedipe* and *Bérénice* were admired and *Mithridate* and *Pulchérie* compared, and there was a little group of provincial *precieuses* who were obstinate in calling the author of *Cinna* "Cléocrite the Elder."[1]

It was, therefore, an eloquent, polite and measured environmène in which one lived in an amiable fashion, submissive to the rules of good society. It did not seem propitious to awaken passions, and above all to nourish them, and if gallantry was practiced there it was a somewhat insipid and already outdated gallantry: an allegorical gallantry that petrified the ardor of sentiments, and which even an appearance of violence would have shocked. Every woman, however, received delicate homages there, such that the virtuous could easily reconcile their virtue with a desire for adulation, so sentimental couples were not rare in Madame de Lomelas' house.

As for her, it seemed that she ought never to inspire sentiments other than those commanded by courtesy. She was above medium height and sufficiently robust for her step to be heavy. Her manner was gauche, and only acquired ease when she spoke. Then she became animated and became almost gracious; her gestures harmonized with her words, taking on amplitude and

1 Pierre Corneille, the author of the tragedy *Cinna*, is credited with the nickname "Cléocrite l'aisne [i.e. the elder] in *Le Grand dictionnaire des prétieuses* (1660, enlarged 1661) by Antoine Baudeau, Sieur de Somaize. "Précieuses" [precious women] was the insulting label attached to those ladies of the salon culture of Louis XIV's court who were gifted with exceptional intelligence and wit; they were prone to disguise the people they were mocking with pseudonyms; one of the most important *précieuses* was Madame de Scudéry, who based many of the characters in her novels on notable contemporaries; Cléocrite appears in her exceedingly long novel *Artamène, ou le grand Cyrus* (1654).

nobility. In discussion, her face, which was rude and masculine, lit up. Her dark eyes shone with intelligence, her fleshy and gracious mouth smiled mischievously and she became almost seductive. When one was admitted to her intimacy, one savored in her company the satisfaction that intelligent and alert amity procures, and a becoming generosity.

Among the few intimates that were able to penetrate her home at any hour was a President of the Chambre des Comptes named La Grille. When he met Madame de Lomelas, President La Grille was already in his forties; he was married and the father of two children. He was a pious man, but not devout, and highly literate; he was both a jurisconsultant and a poet, he translated psalms in verse and composed rather well-turned epistles.

An amiable conversationalist, he had a witty repartee and a keen sense of humor, and yet, when the conversation turned to matters of amour, he revealed himself to be a sentimentalist; his customarily clear and well-pitched voice was veiled and became caressant and tender. It was noticeable, however, that when Monsieur de La Grille gave his opinion on amorous controversies, Madame de Lomelas listened more attentively than she ordinarily listened to the other contributors, and her face then took on the seductive softness that was only seen when she spoke. She gazed at the President with a singular ardor and when he warmed up while arguing, he could not help turning his gaze toward her.

Nevertheless, although La Grille and Madame de Lomelas were not always able to hide the extreme pleasure they experienced in one another's company, the familiars of the house were strangers to veritable passion to such a degree that none of them thought of wondering what the nature of the sympathy was that those two individuals testified to one another. They were, in any case, both above suspicion. The ugliness of Madame de Lomelas was a guarantee to which La Grille's piety responded and they were both held to be model spouses.

In spite of those appearances, they loved one another profoundly, and if they were able to conceal their amour so skillfully from all eyes it was not by virtue of hypocrisy but in order not to permit malignity to soil their tenderness.

They had known one another for ten years when Madame de Lomelas died. Le Grille's grief was such that it was scarcely possible to attribute it to the chagrin of having lost a friend. There was much talk about it, and the absolute retreat to which the President confined himself increased suspicions; people tried to remember facts that might serve as proofs, but the conduct of the lovers had been so perfect that no one could find even the appearance of one. It was La Grille who provided it himself, in a tragic fashion.

The death of Madame de Lomelas had been a frightful blow for him; he had devoted his mind, heart and senses to her to such an extent that her disappearance was unbearable to him. As he was religious, he tried to resist his dolor; he told himself that his duty was to remain with his wife and children; he appealed to all the resources of his faith, but it was in vain. Of his beliefs he only retained one thing: the hope of one day seeing his mistress again and of being united with her, even at the price of a thousand torments.

When the idea that he might see her again had entered into him, it invaded him entirely, and he had no other desire than that of abandoning a life that had become odious to him. He struggled thus for six months, prey to the most frightful tortures, and one day he decided to die. However, as soon as he had made that decision, doubt seized him, which was a new torture for him, more terrible than all those to which he had been subjected. His certitude of seeing his lover abandoned him, but he had lost the will to live and already belonged to death.

He did not even have the courage to renounce his design, and an irresistible and abominable desire became the sole mistress of his being; in the midst of the anguish of his doubt, the intense, poignant desire to see Madame de Lomelas again took possession of him, and he understood that it would be necessary for him to satisfy it. He did not hesitate. Madame de Lomelas had been buried by the Capuchins; La Grille solicited from them the authorization to have the coffin opened, and obtained that favor.

The people who witnessed that scene conserved such an unforgettable memory of it that it has been transmitted, as poignantly, to all the hearers of this story.

When Madame de Lomelas' coffin was opened, it was seen that the dead woman no longer had anything but one hand intact, and all those present, even the monks recoiled; but La Grille seemed to be insensible to the frightful odor that the putrescence exhaled; he did not see anything but that white and beautiful hand; he fell upon it, kissed it piously and passionately, shedding tears, and the others had difficulty dragging him away from that frightful kiss.

When the coffin was nailed shut again, La Grille thanked the Capuchins and asked them to bury him, when he died, beside Madame de Lomelas. Having obtained that assurance from them, he left.

The next day, as he had not reappeared at his home, a search was mounted for him throughout Montpellier, and his body was found, in the evening, in a little stream near the town.

In the sight of his lover, perhaps he had once again drawn the hope of seeing her again, or perhaps it had sufficed for him to kiss one last time, before dying, that perishable flesh, a parcel of which seemed to have been conserved for his lips.

Doubt

"I'VE been thinking about the story you told us yesterday, Anselme," said Nalle.

"And what do you think of it?"

"I think that La Grille wasn't excessively tormented by his doubts. His hesitations were brief, and I imagine that things don't always happen as simply, or that one can resolve them with the same clarity that characterized Madame de Lomelas' lover."

"You're not wrong. It's nevertheless true that La Grille couldn't have acted differently; he was a literate and passionate man, not a theologian or a metaphysician; let us even say that, deep down, he was a rationalist, or a man capable of satisfying himself at scant expense. I've encountered people who were far less prompt to calm their apprehensions, especially a woman whose life story I want to tell you, Nalle, for you'll appreciate its disorder."

"You knew the woman in question?"

"I once found myself in her presence."

"Where?"

"In a lunatic asylum that I had occasion to visit, the medical director of which I knew. He wanted to take me to see his population of shades, and, in a few brief sentences, he introduced those demented individuals to me. Few among them retained me, for their follies were as vulgar as the wisdom can be of many people to whom one attributes a plentitude of reason. One woman, however, attracted my gaze, and appeared to me to be elevated above her companions in misery. She might have been about forty, but her hair was completely white, and thus matched her bloodless and exhausted face, with delicate features that were elongated, as her entire slender body seemed to be. She was sitting on a bench, her hands joined and her gaze ecstatic.

"'What about that one?' I asked the doctor. 'Religious folly?'

"'Yes and no,' replied the doctor; when we've concluded your visit, I'll tell you her story.'

"We continued to wander through that land of darkness, and when, already sickened by sadness, I got back to my friend's study, he kept his promise and told me the following story."

The woman you noticed is named Madame Bettina Laflorence, and it's already three years since she was brought to this refuge, from which she will probably never emerge except to conquer the even more reliable peace of death. It was me who brought her here, because she has no family; I had known her for many years;

I've followed the phases of her illness and I foresaw the outcome, so I can talk to you about her.

She is the daughter of a doctor of philosophy, professor in some German university, Otto Reiwarthner, a widower who brought up his only child in the study of philosophers and theologians. At nineteen years of age Mademoiselle Reiwarthner was able to sustain a thesis. She was passionate about the mystics of all ages, from Plotinus to Swedenborg, and future human destinies already preoccupied her at an age when young girls have scarcely ceased opening the bellies of their dolls, which is their fashion of metaphysics in searching for the soul.

When the worthy Reiwarthner died, Bettina was twenty-one years old. On his deathbed, her father had begged her not to live alone and to marry one of his pupils, a Frenchman, Monsieur Laflorence, in whom she had inspired a profound passion. Out of deference to that parental last wish, she married the young man, who had just been appointed a lecturer in a Faculty. Bettina did not love her husband; she was, however, an excellent wife for him and wept appropriately when he died four years after their marriage.

Still young, of a very tender and pure beauty, she was courted, and was not insensible to the attentions of one of her admirers. She loved profoundly, with all the impetuosity of a virgin soul that the labor of thought had neither dried up not satisfied. Fate was cruel to her; a week before the wedding, her lover suddenly passed away. She remained cloistered for a long time, dead to joy and to sorrow, buried beneath the ruins of a happiness all the more beautiful because it had only been glimpsed.

The necessities of existence obliged her to emerge from her retreat. Devoid of fortune, she gave piano lessons in order to live, and, in order to escape her chagrin, she plunged herself once again into her favorite studies.

Considering her life as closed and henceforth devoid of purpose, she interrogated herself regarding the mysterious future that awaits beings, and was troubled by the eventual revivification. She believed firmly in survival, but what troubled her was the nature of that survival. She sought an answer to that problem, by turns, in Buddhist and Pythagorean transmigration, in Stoic palingenesis, in the Alexandrian emanation and a return to the supreme source. Not being satisfied by the metaphysicians, she slowly returned to the Catholicism of her childhood; converted doctrinally by the fathers of the Church, she gradually sensed her faith becoming firmer and confessed her belief in the immortality of the soul and the individual personality.

From then on, as soon as she had faith, she knew doubt, that child of religions. One thought commenced to obsess her. If, after centuries, she returned in the new heaven of which Isaiah, Saint John and Saint Peter had spoken, how would she find herself in regard to the two men to whom she had belonged? Toward which would she go? Toward the one who had had her flesh, or the one who had had her heart?

All her subtleties, and all the resources of her theological science were impotent to give her peace. The question posed itself incessantly, and she saw no possible outcome. One day, while reading the Gospel, she came across the story of the woman about whom the Sadducees spoke to Jesus. She had married seven brothers, and the Sadducees asked of which of the seven she would be the wife after the resurrection. Jesus had replied: "In the time of the resurrection there will be neither husbands nor wives, but they will be like God's angels in heaven."

Bettina saw that as a revelation; for some months she rediscovered peace, but then she was assailed by doubt again, and her faith, which ordered her to believe, struggled with the memory of her amour, which commanded her to hope for an ultimate union.

Her life then became a perpetual oscillation. Sometimes, faithful to the Church, she returned to the holy text and expiated by fasting the sin of having not believed in the Word. Even at those times, however, her adventurous intelligence carried her away. She wanted to know what the realm was that had been prepared for the blessed since the creation of the world, where the celestial city was, illuminated by the splendor of God, and what her blissful essence would be in the divine circles and on the recreated globe. By turns she obtained replies from Saint Gregory of Nyssa and Saint Augustine, Athenagoras and Tertullian, Cardinal Bellarmine and Dom Calmet, and each one aggravated her anguish. Then she abandoned the canon, the catechism and orthodoxy, and she dreamed about her future conflicts between the husband of her body and the spouse of her thought.

Everything seemed to her, at that moment, to depend on the nature of her soul. Would it be clad in an etheric, subtle matter, and spherical in form, as Chrysippus had said and Origen had repeated? She sometimes said yes, and despaired, convinced that she would belong for eternity to Laflorence if she subsisted materialized in that fashion. She only returned to her lover in thinking about the discourses of the Egyptian Gnostcs, pupils of the monk Hierocas, who affirmed that we would be given and entirely new spiritual body.

At first these crises were separated by fairly long intervals, during which Bettina savored a relative quietude; gradually, they grew closer together, perturbing her faculties and hallucinating her with unusual visions. She dreamed about the earth of the afterlife, wondering whether it would be a transformation of our present dwelling or whether the celestial bodies would be part of that glorious empire.

She remained motionless for two entire days, sitting in a dark corner of her room, forgetting to take any nourishment, her being extended toward distant realms. She thought about the mysterious abode about which the ancient Persians already spoke, the abode in which the psalmist believed when he sang about the heavens of the heavens that are the Lord's. Eyes fixed, she saw the vault of crystal, enveloped itself by the empyrean heaven, the seat of the glory of God and the elect, continuing the planets and the fixed stars, the description of which she had read in Thilo.[1] Then everything changed and she perceived the immense star, the common center of all the stellar system, an unusual and marvelous realm, an ineffable palace of divinity.

---

1 Bishop Thilo of Trotha (1466-1514).

Everywhere she saw herself with the adored, living the life that she had not lived, and when she returned from her ecstasies she fell into a frightful despair.

She abandoned her pupils, and, having previously taken so much care of her person, she neglected to maintain the remains of her touching beauty. She wandered through the streets, stammering vague words, her eyes empty and her hands trembling. She often stopped, immobilizing her face, which was animated by a poignant smile, proffering a name that no one heard. One day, she was seen running through the streets of the city, unkempt, howling, her features convulsed with horror and fear, crying that she had lost her beloved forever.

I had her bought to this house; she vociferated for many weeks, and then, one day, abruptly, when I went in to see her, she said to me: "I've found him again." Since then, she's been as you've seen her; in the night of the mind, she has found peace; she is dead-alive, and her hours pass in the company of her lover. No one has heard her pronounce a syllable since; her lips agitate, for she converses, naturally, with the lover who has returned, and perhaps she will only wake from her dream when the hour of her death is imminent.

"It's necessary not to wish for that," said Nalle, "for why destroy the happiness that she has edified with such difficulty? Why make her quit the port that she has found, better than the unfortunate La Grille? I want to hope that she never recovers her reason."

Delilah

"*SAMSON VANQUISHED*, Lary's last painting," replied Anselme, in answer to Nalle's question. "When he finished it—he was thirty years old—the old master stopped painting, and went to sleep alive in his glory."

"He was a sage," said Nalle.

"Perhaps," said Anselme.

"What do you mean?"

"Look at the painting again and I'll answer you."

In a narrow courtyard with cyclopean walls—a sort of ditch that an enormous somber arch connected to mysterious and sinister galleries designed in the distance behind the sullen stones—Samson was represented turning a mill. His head was shaven by slaves and his red eyes illuminated his face with unknown fires. He, the robust, was toiling rudely; his muscles were inflated over his breast and arms, and one divined that they were weak and impotent; sweat was trickling down his brow and the nails of his clenched fingers were bloody and broken. His formidable body seemed to have collapsed, and one divined the soft flesh that was accumulating slowly; the legs were wobbling; the knees, doubtless torn by falls or involuntary friction, were bumping into one another.

From the man's face, however, in spite of the torture and the dolor, a profound joy emanated, lubricating the features that suffering had not succeeded in contracting: a joy capable of transfiguring the pale face and softening the terrible pupils devoid of a gaze. Samson seemed happy, and the artist had shown him at the moment when a frisson of more intense felicity gripped him and immobilized him, the instant when his floating tunic brushed the shoulders of a woman sitting on the ground and looking at him: Delilah.

The splendor of the woman filled the entire canvas. The hair thick, the head supported by the two cupped hands, the superb young body leaning forward, she was voluptuousness and beauty. Her sharp eyes, pensive and sad, were gazing at the captive, and they were full of infinite love, penetrated by soft flames, benevolent stars illuminating the darkness of the vanquished. Simultaneously servant and mistress, triumphant and submissive, victorious and defeated, she was crouching in the depths of the quarry, hallucinated by the spectacle provided to her by the man she had tamed.

"Did you know Lary?" Nalle asked, when he had contemplated the masterpiece for a long time.

"I knew him, and he was the one who gave me that canvas, a precious gift of his amity and an inestimable testimony of his suffering and his happiness. You've understood the symbolism?"

"I don't believe I've understood it perfectly. Doubtless Lary met a woman one day and that woman was able to conquer his heart and his amour. She made him renounce that which was not her, she knew the secret of his strength as a dreamer, and artist, a creator of phantoms; she destroyed his power and substituted the cult of her beauty, her flesh and her mind for the cult of vain and beautiful forms that he was able to animate . . . Perhaps that's it. But then, why the joy of the vanquished and the tenderness of the executioner, and what is she doing next to the man that is being tortured?"

"I asked those questions one summer evening of old Lary. He was at his home, in the country, in a remote corner of Provence where he ended his life. When, like you, I had admired the work, I told him that I did not grasp its meaning entirely. I confessed to him that the presence of the woman, above all, confused me. In what antique legendary treasury had he read that Delilah had not fled the man she had betrayed?

"'You believe then, that she abandoned him after the princes of the Philistines had bound his arms and chained his body?' he said. 'Take that old Bible and read me the story; I like it best of all.'

I picked up the book and I read. Lary listened to me silently and didn't interrupt me until I reached the verse: *After that he loved a woman in the valley of Sorah.*

"'He loved her more,' he said, 'than he loved the weak and stupid virgin of Thimus who was his first wife, for Delilah was a woman with all her mystery. The poet does not say that she was beautiful; one does not say that of beauty; he does not say that she was desirable, one does not say that even of lust; he does not say that she was more attractive than the eyes of the sea; one cannot say that of seduction.'

94

He fell silent and I continued, and when I came to the words spoken by Delilah: "She said to him 'How can you say: *I love you*, since your heart is not with me?'" Lary stopped me again.

"'She was right,' he murmured. 'He did not love her, since he deceived her in his secret thoughts, since he hid a part of himself from her, and the book is wrong to say that Samson was "vexed unto death." He understood, on the contrary, that his true life would commence on the day when he was sincere with the one he had chosen as his companion, and he let her withdraw from him, not his body—how clear the symbolism is!—but his soul, everything that was foreign to his amour. And when she had taken from the man she loved the seven tresses of his head, when she had delivered him from the seven vices of his flesh and his spirit, Samson became blind—which is to say that he no longer understood the vanities of before, the chimerical pride, the follies of the spirit—and he accepted to turn the rude mill of life.'

"'He was alone then,' I said to Lary, 'for henceforth the Bible makes no further mention of Delilah; she disappears, and after her victory she enters into the shadows.'

"'Why speak of her, since she has accomplished her work? But what a vulgar soul it is necessary to have not to understand that she loved, with an amour as tender and profound as the night, the man that she had liberated from the chimera, the man to whom she had given the intense joy of living, like everyone else, the good, warm and cheerful life; the man for whom she had been the torch and the cup, the breath of pure air and the caress of the sun?'

"As Lary spoke those words I saw coming into the room where we were the woman who had been his companion for twenty years, and by the gazes that the two of them exchanged, I understood everything."

Conversion

A few years ago, traveling on foot in England, I stopped in Huntingdon and forgot myself there for a few days, resting from my forced march, having nothing to occupy my mind but the memory of Cromwell, who departed from there obscure, to kill and to reign.

After a week of inaction, I resumed short vagabondages though the pastures and walks along the banks of the Ouse, whose waters snaked through the countryside. An old peasant, a hardened poacher, had appointed himself my guide, and during the idle afternoons he told me his adventures or a few tales: old legends of the region or chapters from the local chronicle, the estimable rebel could tell them well, and more than one of those stories has remained in my memory.

One morning, as we followed the thread of the Ouse, musing near the bank, we passed the normal terminus of our excursions and our boat stopped near a large town perched on a hill that overlooked the river. On the bank at the bottom of the hill, a hospitable tavern was open, and, as it was too late to go back to

Huntingdon, we moored the boat, and were soon installed under an arbor in front of a tankard of ale and bloody roast beef.

After a few moments consecrated to satisfying his robust appetite, which had been further exasperated by the morning breeze, Keen, my companion, leaning back against the wall, uttered a joyful exclamation and declared: "I didn't know that one could eat so well in such a place as this."

Surprised by the unusual remark, I replied. "I don't see, Keen, anything extraordinary about this place."

"Because you don't know," he retorted, ambiguously.

"I'd like to know, then."

"Do you think that one can expect anything good from a place in which you won't find a single Christian, no matter how hard you look?"

"Certainly not," I replied. "But what heretics inhabit this town?"

"Papists, sir—Catholics, as they call themselves. Isn't it a pity, for true Englishmen?"

With an energetic *hum* I endorsed Keen; I knew he was fastidious, and I did not want to alienate my companion.

"It astonishes you," he said, "to find such a colony in this country?"

I confessed with a good grace that my curiosity was awakened. "You, who know everything, Keen," I said, flattering him shamelessly, "can't be unaware of the circumstances that brought that tribe to the banks of the Ouse."

"Yes, it's a very old story."

He lit his earthenware pipe, put his elbows on the table and, without being invited, began. Such as he told it to me, I shall repeat that improbable and naïve legend.

It was under I don't know what king, and the souls of this village were administered by the rector John Harnfax. Harnfax was a knowledgeable man, whom, some said, bishops and doctors came to consult. Others said, it's true, that he was a simpleton and had only ever read the Bible. I don't really believe that, for the Bible is an excellent book, and if Harnfax had only read that, he wouldn't have turned out badly afterwards.

What's certain is that he was a model of virtue. He never drank, only ate boiled vegetables, fasted on Sunday and spent the greater part of his time meditating profoundly. Doubtless he paused a little to dream at night, for Mrs. Harnfax had had twelve children by him, twelve boys, all vigorous, healthy and pretending to fear God.

He was well liked by his parishioners, who, touched by his sobriety, moved by his mortifications, considered him as a saint. They even attributed a prophetic gift to him, believing him to be inspired, and he had acquired the greatest influence over them.

For years, Harnfax lived in his deanery, fulfilling the functions of his ministry, preaching, baptizing, marrying and burying his flock. He had talents as an orator and people came from neighboring villages to hear him preach.

One thought, however, troubled the rector. He had a pitying soul, and only thought with a frightful pain in the heart about the host of people deprived of the light of the true faith. The idea that thousands of people condemned themselves benevolently to damnation and frightful tortures haunted his mind, and he would have sacrificed his tranquility willingly for the salvation of his brethren.

Those sentiments, in a clergyman, were quite natural, even praiseworthy, but Harnfax exaggerated them. He soon declared that the only cause of the evils of the world was the diversity of sects that divided humanity. According to him, the unanimous adoption of one confession ought to lead to universal happiness.

Harnfax, who had mystical inclinations, didn't take long to believe that he was destined by God for the role of confessor of nations. He affirmed to several of his intimates that he had been favored by special revelations, and let it be understood that before long he would expose in the pulpit a project capable of moving the earth and leading it to perfect felicity.

His friends, anxious about his excitement, and fearing that he was heading for disaster, tried to distract him from his preoccupations. Their solicitude was in vain, and one Sunday, before all his faithful, Harnfax spoke.

He talked, in such a fashion that his listeners shuddered, about the calamities that overwhelm our planet; he evoked the wars, famines and pestilences that desolate nations, and made a frightful tableau of those plagues of Egypt. He saw the cause of those miseries in the divergence of religious confessions, which he proposed to bring back to unity.

Convinced of the efficacy of his remedy, he had long sought the means to apply it, surely and rapidly. He affirmed that it was not sufficient to send our priests to catechize savage tribes, which are more disposed to cut off the ears, noses and worse off our envoys than to render to their objurgations. The conversion of those peoples, in any case, wouldn't bring any great change to our mores.

"What is important is to bring back to us the European states corrupted by Papism, or the errors of Luther and Calvin, and there, I scarcely believe in individual action, for, if not tortures, at least insults and humiliations would be lavished on our missionaries; they would be the butt of the most bitter mockery, and their urbanity would inevitably be more harmful than useful.

"It would be necessary, to persuade the horde of the incredulous and the sons of Belial, that the Lord himself consented to appear to them and promulgate his eternal will. I imagine that it isn't in the Lord's designs to intervene; if he had been inclined to do so, the ardent prayers that I've addressed to him for a long time would have incited him to depart from his silence.

"Perhaps, confident in his own wisdom, knowing that the day of unanimous reconciliation will come, he considers that the date, near or distant, is unimportant, since the hour must sound.

"It is therefore necessary to renounce acting upon the divinity, but you are not unaware that millions of our fellows are inclining before a man that they consider to be the representative down here of Jesus. The desires and orders of that man they must obey with humility; they listen to his sovereign voice and he is the one who directs their conscience and their heart.

"It is to that man that it is necessary to go; it is to his ears that it is necessary to proffer the words of truth, and, rather than the Hurons or the Iroquois, it is the Pope himself that it is necessary to convert."

✳

"You see, sir," Keen observed, "that Harnfax was nothing but a madman."

"A wretched madman, assuredly," I replied.

"How, though, can a madman be kept from following his madness?" Keen said, and continued.

✳

All that Harnfax's friends and relatives could say, all the objections they found, all the supplications to which they descended, were futile, and one morning, the Reverend set off for Rome, with no luggage but his big Bible with a silver clasp. Confident in God, he didn't even want to take a penny with him.

How did he live on the way? The local people claim that an angel brought him his daily nourishment every morning, but one can't lend credit to what they say.

At any rate, he arrived in Rome, and, straight away, he went to the Vatican. To the guards that stopped him he affirmed that Jesus had sent him, and he asked to speak to the Pope. Which one was it? I don't know. They didn't want to listen to him, and he quickly realized that one doesn't get into the palace as one goes into his presbytery.

For months he exhausted himself taking steps, requesting an audience, heaping archbishops and cardinals with petitions, exposing his intentions in interminable supplications. Soon he was well-known in Rome; people pointed him out, while he visited churches and allowed his eyes and ears to be seduced by Catholic pomp. People whispered: "That's the man who has come from England to convert our Holy Father the Pope."

He even stirred up the devout, and one evening, attacked in a square, he thought that he had found the martyrdom that he wasn't seeking.

Meanwhile, the Pontiff, who had learned about his arrival, touched by his obstinacy, wanted to see him. Harnfax, radiant with beatitude, went into the Vatican, which he had come to conquer.

What happened between him and the Pope no one ever knew exactly. What is certain is that Harnfax worked very insistently on his interlocutor. If one can believe his admirers, the Pope even assured him that only worldly proprieties prevented him from acceding to his desire.

As for the fundamentals, he confessed that Harnfax's opinion was sound, and that the adoption of one faith among those who governed men was the sole means of arriving at human bliss—except that he couldn't see why the Roman Church should bow down before the Anglican, and, according to him, it was much simpler to bring the world back to Catholicism, Catholicism having more adherents.

Struck by those objections, Harfax asked to reflect. Benevolently, the Pope confided him to shrewd Jesuits, and after two months of meditation and solitude, Harnfax, having seen the Pope again, returned to England, where he began the universal conversion with the conversion of his parishioners, who had the custom of listening to him blindly.

✳

"And that's why," Keen added, "the county is afflicted by these people, who dry up the crops when they walk along the edges of our fields."

For the last time, he emptied his tankard of ale, and shook his head as we went back to the boat.

"I'd have thought them more like to give us frog rum than such good ale," he concluded.

The worthy Keen was ignorant of tolerance, and the unitary folly of the Reverend Harnfax irritated him, because he would have liked the entire world to be Wesleyan like him.

Prospero's Flight

" AND you met him?" asked Nalle.

"Yes," replied Anselme.

"Yesterday, the day of Mardi Gras?"

"Yesterday, indeed."

"You talked to him?"

"We chatted together."

"And it was really him?"

"It was him."

"Him, the divine Prospero."

"Why do you call him divine? He was Prospero, Duke of Milan."

"How did you recognize him?"

"I didn't recognize him, since I'd never seen him before that moment; I divined that it was him."

"Wasn't he wearing a mask?"

"Possibly, Nalle, but what does it matter, since, even so, I assure you, he had the soul and the mind of the old Duke."

"Tell me what he said, then."

"I'll tell you what we talked about."

I encountered Prospero as dawn was breaking outside the Opéra; he was alone and seemed melancholy. He was dressed like his godfather Shakespeare, such as the statue in the Boulevard Haussmann presents him to our admiration, which seems, in its meditative attitude, to be seeking a means of quitting its pedestal and going to sit down near the ruins in the Parc Monceau, on the edge of the lake—a propitious place for dreaming, which the good Will would doubtless like to frequent, while dreaming about Stratford. But the Duke's doublet was in a very poor condition, frayed, even torn, and soiled with mud. Perhaps the noble lord had been assailed by a gang of discourteous masks.

I was slightly surprised to find him there, in such a wretched get-up, and without his presence being astonishing. I advanced toward him, and after a rapid introduction I asked him for permission to chat with him. He granted it to me with a perfect grace, inasmuch as he mistook me for a reporter, and told me that he was not a man to scorn modern customs. "Besides which," he added, "I've always occupied myself with a little magic and I've often had occasion to interrogate the illustrious dead after having evoked them."

I didn't want to disabuse him, because his error was doubtless the cause of his benevolence; I concluded that the good Duke didn't detest publicity, and that he was a little like all traveling princes.

"Are you alone in Paris?" I asked him.

"I've been alone for a long time," Prospero replied. "My courtiers have abandoned me, Miranda is dead,

Caliban has fled and I'm told that he's the President of a Republic. That doesn't surprise me; he could only turn out badly. Stephano and that mooncalf Trinculo have remained faithful to me, though; they cheer me up, and I beat them from time to time to distract myself. They wanted to accompany me to Paris, where I'm only passing through on my way to London."

"What have you done with those two companions?"

"They spotted a bodega this evening and I couldn't dissuade them from going in. They must be distracting themselves there drinking sack and a few pints of huff-cap;[1] they'll only come out with full bellies and their heads spinning like parish tops, as Will put it. They've already caused a scandal at the Opéra on Saturday dancing a Moorish dance and they surprised the audience by shouting at the top of their voices for the May Queen and Tom the Piper, or, for want of them, Robin Hood and Maid Marian. I'm not sorry to be rid of their noisy company; it puts me at my ease to talk to you. On what subject would you like to interrogate me?"

"I'd like to ask you your opinions on the social question, but, apart from the fact that it would take us too far away, I believe that you've never been up to date with economic questions, and one of our best philosophers, Ernest Renan, has even observed that you lack practical sense."

---

1 *Trousse-chapeau* [huff-cap] is named by several French sources, including an 1893 study of Shakespeare by the Belgian Symbolist Georges Eekhoud, as a kind of strong beer, but in the original Shakespearean text (*Henry IV, Part One*) Pistol uses it metaphorically to refer to boasting, and its usual literal reference in English is to a kind of mushroom.

"I didn't like the book by Monsieur Renan to which you're alluding," the Duke replied, coldly.[1] "I haven't put it in my library."

I nodded my head, and in order not to offend him, I didn't try to pursue the argument. As a gang of drunken dock-workers were going past, I said to him: "What do you think of our Carnival?"

"Yours?"

"Ours, if you please."

"Do you call a Carnival that lugubrious file of shop-soiled Pierrots, tinpot Harlequins and deplorable Columbines? Add that sinister promenade of a sad crowd, waiting for a spectacle that doesn't arrive, has never arrived and never will arrive, but wandering even so through the boulevard and the streets, convinced of the futility of its expectation—is that a Carnival too?"

"That's our Carnival," I replied, "and you've observed our rejoicing on that day accurately."

"You have no Carnival," Prospero affirmed. "For you, Carnival is a date, not a fête, much less an institution."

"An institution? What do you mean by that?" I asked, not without surprise.

"I'll tell you, inasmuch as it's connected to the history of the Duchy of Milan—and it's an unpublished page that I'll give you. It will permit you to clarify certain events that remain obscure, in spite of the great Shakespeare—and even Monsieur Renan," he added, ironically. "Do you know why I was expelled from Milan?"

---

1 Ernest Renan's *Caliban: Suite de la Tempête, Drame Philosophique* (1878).

I confessed my ignorance; my professors had always neglected to entertain me with those historical details.

"This is what happened," said the Duke, benevolently. "Since I had attained the age of reason, the Carnival had always been one of my principal preoccupations. I'm one of those people who claim that even the most seemingly futile things sometimes contain a profound verity. In my opinion the fantastic whim that impels people, once a year, to dress up, must have an ancient origin, and it must have been serious motives that led ancient peoples to promote those celebrations and masquerades.

"In brief, the Carnival must certainly have had the aim, in the beginning, of symbolizing some true idea, or some dogma. Evidently priestly in origin, it had rapidly fallen into the hands of the people, had been perverted and had lost its reason for being. The principles that presided over its origin had been forgotten, and a ceremony that was probably religious or moral had been made into a burlesque comedy.

"I applied myself for many years to rediscovering the meaning of the Carnival, and after fruitful reflections, I thought that I had found it."

"What is it?" I asked, intrigued.

"The philosophers of old," Prospero continued, "being subtle observers, had not taken long to perceive that dissimulation alone regulated the relationships between human beings. From childhood on they were accustomed to conceal their veritable sentiments, disguise their intimate thoughts, veil their passions and hide their vices. They were educated every day in the art of masking themselves and thus being able to deceive and abuse one another. At first, they only put on those parade costumes in certain determined circumstances, when it was necessary to obtain, either from the gods or from their neighbors, some favor that their merit was insufficient to procure. Gradually, by force of habit, enchained by bonds that they had prepared, they affected for themselves the attitudes that they adopted before others, and almost forgot their true nature.

"In order to obviate such deadly mores, the sages decided that every year, for a few days, the citizens of towns—the evil had not reached the countryside—would be obliged to dress in costumes appropriate to their true essence, and would be constrained during that brief period to appear as they really were, so that for a few brief hours one could see one's relatives, friends and even indifferent individuals without the masks that they normally wore.

"Those precepts were followed for a long time; then, either because of forgetfulness or because people were obliged to increasingly great efforts in order to rid themselves of their chosen disguises and rediscover their true image, the laws that had been promulgated were no longer observed; the Carnival was retained, but it was no longer what it had been and what it ought to have been.

"In possession of that certainty, I wanted to restore the rational Carnival within my estates. I published an edict; it prescribed the new mode of the festivals and the penalties that would be inflicted on rebels. My people, faithful until then, could not abide the idea of showing themselves without borrowed ornaments, and especially not that of confronting themselves. Very shrewd courtiers urged me to withdraw my edict; I refused, in order to demonstrate the value of my authority, and two days later, my subjects revolted, and expelled me from Milan."

Duke Prospero stopped. The memories he had just recalled were so cruel for him that he collapsed on a bench, covered his face and started sobbing. I did not want to trouble his dolor; without a word, discreetly, I abandoned him, and I headed for Les Halles, expecting to find Trinculo and Stephano in some tavern.

"Did you find them?" asked Nalle.

"Alas, no, my friend, any more than I found Prospero again."

The King's Refusal

"I adore fairy tales," said Nalle.

"Why?" asked Anselme. "Is it for love of the chimerical or the absurd?"

"No, it's not for that, and I'm not like our friend Marc, who likes tales all the more if they're illogical or implausible, pretending to relax thus from the rigors of dialectics. I cherish fables when they're vague and imprecise, when I can group a thousand adventitious dreams around them, a thousand adjacent imaginations. Then, for me, they're what hashish and opium are for so many others—less perfidious and less dangerous hashish and opium. They become friends, mild and benevolent stimulants. I charge them with my visions and my dreams, as spinners load their distaffs with yarn woven by unknown weavers, and it's from them that I draw the thread of my thoughts and my dreams. So I need them taut and murky, light and fluid, such that they can't constrain my vagabond, fugitive and free desires. Tell me a tale, Anselme."

"It won't please you, my good Nalle."

"Tell it anyway."

"All right."

Anselme collected himself momentarily, and then began: "There was once a king . . ."

"And a queen who had no children," Nalle interrupted. "Oh, Anselme, do you take me for a child that one can satisfy with mere nutshells?"

Untroubled, Anselme continued.

"He was the king of a little-known country, of which the subtlest and best informed historians are unaware; a country flourishing with splendid gardens, covered in woods and boscage, which extended to the shore of the sea. On the edge of the sea there was the city where the king ruled."

"And the city was made of marble?" asked Nalle. "One saw nothing there but terraces of porphyry, and colonnades of jasper, and palaces clad in gold, on the rooftops of which dragons and chimeras palpitated. Don't describe that city for me, Anselme. I know every last corner of it, and I'm weary of it; its splendors have fatigued my senses too often and I prefer the vague city of the Opium-Eater."

"It wasn't a city of gold and silver, Nalle," Anselme replied. "It was a town rather than a capital, and I don't know how to tell you what that town was like. I imagine that there were low and rather somber houses there, confused intersections, and narrow back-streets, very dark and very dirty, which seemed to lose themselves in the distance. In the evening, they extended infinitely, for at the end of each one the sea could be seen, on all sides, I believe, for I remember now that the town was built on an island, and when I attach my imagination to that island, I can see it drawing away out to sea, and there are no longer gardens and woods around it; it's a

113

lost island, solitary, stirred by the alternately supple and furious voice of the wind. Look! Do you see, now that I'm trying to depict them, that the city and the island are misting over, and that fuliginous shadows are wandering through the streets, all the way to the strand."

"I've often thought about a similar country, Anselme," said Nalle. "I'm not sure, even now, that I wasn't born a subject of your king; in any case, I'd be glad to become one."

"Have I told you that the king was melancholy?"

"I guessed it, and that's why I cherish him."

"So, the king was melancholy, but, at the time when my story begins, he was only melancholy because his ancestors had always been thus."

"A powerful reason, Anselme. I'm only so dreamy because my grandfather was a lunatic."

"That's true, Nalle, but what I mean by that is that the young king hadn't yet had any misfortune or chagrin sufficiently precise for him to be able to attach his melancholy to it."

"A fortunate king, since his sadness was virginal!"

"A fortunate king, indeed, but he was unaware of his good fortune, and he was anxious because his languor had no cause."

"He hadn't been in love, then?"

"He was in love. I won't tell you with whom, or how he met her, nor what he said to her the first time they met, nor what he repeated the twentieth time. Know that he got married to please his subjects and to please the princess he had chosen."

"I can see clearly, Anselme; she must have been a petite, thin woman with a sight squint, but beautiful all the same; she had pretty grasping hands, spidery hands; I've known princesses in dreams who had hands like that; they're excellent hands that sometimes seize hearts perfectly. I can see the king's wife quite clearly. She certainly had hair the color of rust, thick and very heavy, and she pinned it up in such a fashion as to have the prow of a ship behind her head. She was clad in a robe the color of the weather: foggy weather, dirtied by rain and sea-spray, or even the smoke of factories."

"The king's wife was indeed petite; she did have hair the color of rust and a slight squint."

"Don't tell me any more of your story, then, Anselme; I know it and I must have encountered that queen. She was very wicked and full of seduction; her flesh was tender and her heart detestable; the king loved her very much, but she didn't love the king and she deceived him, doubtless with an old warrior, not because she loved the warrior but because she knew that the blow would thus be harder for her husband. When I said that I knew that adventure . . . ! Was I wrong?"

"You were right, Nalle, and I won't have to tell you that the king was very unhappy, and that he was also satisfied, because his sadness was no longer without a cause."

"That king was a fool, but I don't blame him, for in his place, I'd have prostituted my melancholy too. But finish your tale."

"You don't know how it ends then?"

"There are several endings. I'd rather hear yours. I think, though, that the king was able to bear the queen's treason."

"He bore it until the day the queen died, and on that day the king was broken by anguish, because he had always cherished the woman who tortured him."

"Naturally, Anselme; and the king couldn't survive his dolor, and he drowned himself one day in order to rejoin his beloved."

"No, the king lived, he lived with his dolor."

"That's the end of your story? That's not a fairy tale."

"Wait! My tale has only begun. The king, who was eaten away by despair, had the custom of going to wander on the sea shore, where his sobs accompanied the plaint of the waves. While contemplating the infinite swell, he felt more alone, and free to moan. One evening, while he was sitting on a rock, he saw a woman coming out of the sea . . ."

"It was the sea lady!"

"If you like. The woman approached the king, who showed no surprise at her presence; she sat down next to him and that she had taken pity on his tears and wanted to help him. As the king shook his head, she let him know that she was a fay, and to do that she made a sign that attracted sirens and dolphins to the beach. The king being convinced of her power, she proposed to take him to a realm of delights where he would not know woe, or chagrin, or death."

"And the king was ecstatic, he accepted, and followed the sea lady."

"No, the king refused. He didn't want to live in a country where woe was unknown, for he had loved the one for whom he was weeping, in good times and bad, and she had shared sweet joys and poisoned pleasures with him. He didn't want to live in a country from

116

which chagrin was banished, for he knew full well that he could only find satisfaction henceforth in the very chagrin that gripped him. He didn't want to live in a country that didn't have death for a sovereign, for, since his beloved had departed, wasn't his sole hope in death?"

"The king wasn't wrong, Anselme, and he was a king I would have loved."

"Are you satisfied with my tale, Nalle?"

"I'm not dissatisfied with it."

Gold

"YES," said Anselme, "in the midst of the rout of all cults, the disarray of all religions and the ruins of all sanctuaries, a single altar has remained standing: that of gold. The old and symbolic Biblical legend is still alive; it survived the collapse of theogonies, dogmas and myths. Gold is still what it was before; it is worshiped, it is cherished, it is conquered like a rude adversary, loved like a mistress; one only separates from it with a broken heart and the secret hope of seeing it again.

"For the men of today, as for those of old, gold is simultaneously the goal and the guide; for the majority of human beings it is the unique ideal: an unappreciable ideal, for one is conscious of the power to attain it. It excites two passions: envy, when one does not have it, jealousy when one does; it favors others, lust and gluttony; it engenders anger and pride.

"It hypnotizes and it dazzles; its yellow flood in the mirror in which millions of beings look at themselves; it absorbs the soul if its followers, and gives them its own; it is the spirit that moves them and vivifies them. Like the antique Jehovah, it is a jealous master, and in

118

the hearts of those who receive it, it kills the weak and compassionate sentiments; its fulgurant gleam closes the eyes to the spectacle of misery and despair; its ring, its sonority, bright or wild, closes the ears to moans of dolor and sobs of distress; it drags in its wake a ferocious and harsh troop who acclaim and insult it by turns, but who only live on it, by it and for it.

"And it isn't only worshipers, its faithful followers, who prostrate themselves at its feet, because it is an existent idol, which can be seen and touched; it also has a priest, and that priest of gold we call a miser. The miser is its true hierophant, the man who is devoted to the God, the man who sacrifices himself to it; he is the pontiff who knows the litanies by which the divinity is touched, and at the same time, he is its slave and its lover.

"The rabble, those who rush to assault the metal, do not know it in its real splendor; interposed between them and it is the cortege of pleasures and mundane joys; they do not see gold in its purity, in its unpolluted radiance, they perceive it with the benefits it supposes, the prebends that it confers, the jubilations that it brings, and for them it is only the supreme procurer, the dispenser of advantages and privileges.

"It seems that an abyss separates that vulgar and sensual mob from the adept who has penetrated and understood the essence of gold, the man who honors the master for itself, who is scornful of any other satisfaction than that of possessing, in a secret and mysterious tabernacle, the almighty image. Nevertheless he is nothing to it; it is among the brutal crowd of pleasure-seekers that gold takes its apostles; it is there that it chooses its fanatics and recruits its proselytes.

"I know the story of one of those conversions; let me tell it to you, and you will understand the bewitching domination of gold and how, after having killed noble thoughts, marvelous ideas and touching virtues, it even arrives at annihilating the vices that it helps to propagate, substituting itself for them and becoming, in the eyes of its believers, the center of everything."

✳

Twenty years ago, I was living in the Rue Lhomond, in one of the old and leprous houses whose bleak and melancholy aspect evoked the idea of some cloister inaccessible to the noises of the world, a place propitious to dreams, where the mind could meditate and isolate itself. Two wings composed the dwelling in question, whose tenants were petty bourgeois, modest rentiers and government employees with exiguous salaries; it was a tranquil population, like a peaceful colony of mollusks, the indifferent life of which could not trouble anyone.

I occupied a small room on the fifth floor from which I rarely emerged, absorbed as I was by study and work, and with the aid of my natural lack of curiosity I stayed there for five years without knowing and perhaps without ever seeing a single one of my neighbors. It is true that the entire floor on which my room was situated remained unoccupied for a long time, to my extreme satisfaction, for I thus had an impression of complete solitude. So, the day when the maidservant who brought my provisions for the day every morning told me that the apartment adjacent to mine had just been let, I was annoyed by it; it seemed to me that strangers were about to impinge upon my life.

They did indeed impinge upon it; their untimely presence agitated me; they solicited my interest by virtue of the very fact that we were living side by side. I thought that if I penetrated their existence, if I knew who they were, I could tolerate their proximity more easily, that they would not be complete strangers to me, and that I would thus avoid threatening perturbations; for, hearing noises so close by was sufficient to deflect my thoughts in their course and introduce unharmonious elements into them. I therefore made enquiries about them.

"It's a household of three persons," the concierge told me, "Madame Darnay, a widow, and her two children, a young man of thirty and a young woman who is scarcely sixteen." She added: "They seem to be very poor." They were undoubtedly a family who had "come down in the world," for their furniture indicated a former but fallen luxury.

She was right, and I was able to convince myself of the fact. The young man, Maurice Darnay—I discovered his name later—went out early in the morning and only came back at night; I assumed that he had some meager employment, on which his mother and sister lived precariously. As for the two women, they never went out, except to fulfill indispensable daily household duties, but they contributed nothing to increase the insufficient resources of which they disposed.

The hazard of encountering them on the stairs or the landing introduced me to them. Madame Darnay was a tall woman, a little stout, with a mild and resigned physiognomy that contrasted with the dolorous face of her daughter, a frail and pale adolescent with a sorrowful and suffering appearance. Maurice was short and thin, with stooped shoulders, a hollow chest, and a ravaged, ferrety face with dull and cold eyes that brief gleams sometimes lit up; he was ordinarily clad in a worn, shiny but sufficiently clean frock-coat; he had a taciturn and apprehensive manner.

They supported their poverty with great dignity, and enclosed themselves in a modest and grim isolation. I admit, to my shame, that it was by means of indiscretions I provoked that I discovered the extent of their deprivation: the hearth sometimes devoid of a fire and the table devoid of bread during the long cold day. I attempted to come to their aid, but they refused all assistance, and I would probably never have learned the frightful drama of their life if I had not found Madame Darnay inanimate on her threshold one evening in December. I picked her up, rang her doorbell violently and, aided by her daughter, carried her to her bed.

It did not take long for me to determine the cause of her faint; she was dying of starvation. A few mouthfuls of broth and a glass of warm Bordeaux were sufficient to reanimate her; she recovered her senses and, on see- ing me beside her she began to sob, while her daughter did her best to calm her down. I was about to withdraw, but she retained me with a gesture, and in a moment of desperate and heart-rending expansion, she made me the confidant of her distress.

She had once been rich, very rich; she had savored all the happiness of which her simple and slightly posi- tive soul dreamed; insouciant about the morrow, she had lived for twenty years in a mild quietude, from which she only emerged on the death of her husband, which left her devoid of resources.

Maurice, who was then eighteen, had only just left the college where he had been educated. He was already a man, according to the formula, one of those practical petty bourgeois, shrewd and resourceful; however, although he was not inclined to reverie and did not allow himself to be lured by chimeras, he had a very keen affection for his mother and sister. He had no other ambition than that of making a fortune, but he associated the people he loved with that ambition. He wanted to be rich, but he only wanted that, to begin with, in order to favor those who lived alongside him, and for whom he desired to reconquer the lost wellbeing.

With that aim, he deprived his youth of all pleasure, weaned himself of all joy. Without respite, he worked with an incredible stubbornness, and, seconded by a special intelligence, and also liberated from all scruples, deaf to all sentimentality, he grew rich after a few years of laborious efforts. But in that enrichment and that progressive hoarding, slowly and insensibly, he forgot his goal.

Very passionate, very sensual and very avid, he promised to compensate himself one day for the ascetic constraint that he had imposed on himself. Gradually, he found his satisfaction in dreaming of future joys, and when the moment came to realize them, he perceived that in his dreams he had taken the edge off all the pleasures to which he could henceforth pretend. Then he preferred to imagine finer, more perfect ones as he acquired more.

The gold he had accumulated, he loved as the latent source of universal joys. Soon, he forgot all the possible delights that the metal encloses; he sensed born in his entrails the love of gold, disengaged from all its contingencies, of all that it might contain of the fragile and the transitory, of pure gold. He knew the intense joy of sensing that he had gold, and he knew the ineffable and terrifying torments of those who fear thieves. He loved gold for itself, for its yellow color, for the beauty of that robe that nothing soils, for its soft and gentle touch, for the sound of its voice, for its indefinable perfume, for the enticing radiance that only misers know.

And gold did its work; in the soul of its priest it killed everything, and the wretch allowed the former tenderness to be extinguished in his heart; he enslaved to his passion those he had cherished, he immolated them to his religion. It is thus that Maurice Darnay, similar to all ferocious believers, sacrificed his own family to the beast that always stands on the unbreakable altar; it was for him, and for the glory of gold, that my neighbors were dying of hunger and misery in the very temple of the idol.

Expiation

MY friend the counselor of justice Justus Raff—I call him my friend although I have only known him for three weeks—was ordinarily a very shrewd old man, clear-minded and imperturbably logical; but when he had drunk a few measures of brown Nürnberg beer, a velvety beer of exquisite taste crowned in glasses with a gilded foam, he became an entirely different man. He revealed himself to be sentimental, mystical, even a trifle hazy, and his positivism escaped in the blue swirls of his pipe. Then the thousand legendary memories of his childhood awoke again in his heart, and the man who, during the day, believed in nothing, not even, undoubtedly, the judgments that he took pleasure in hearing or rendering, was ready to believe in anything.

He lived in Heidelberg and it was there that I met him and linked myself with him. He lived in a little house near the edge of the Neckar, and from his window he could see the path of the philosophers winding over the hill, while he could follow the course of the stream that slithered like a snake among the meadows and the clumps of trees. Every evening I went to look for him; we crossed the river together and, as it was summer, we went to sit under the arbor of a little tavern half way down the hill. There, with Heidelberg and its ivy-enlaced churches at our feet, and the old schloss facing us on the ridge that an age-old blaze has enveloped in melancholy, the two of us chatted in the silence of people and the soft murmur of things.

That evening, Justus was fuller than ever of dreamy humor; perhaps he had drunk excessively and the fumes of his favorite beverage were clouding his brain more. He was not drunk, however, and he would have been very upset if anyone had suspected him of allowing himself to be disconcerted by a few supplementary measures. In any case, the night was propitious to dreams; it was bright and peaceful; the moonlight was bathing the somber fire-trees with candor, its rays were filtering through the woods and coming to spread over the valley, illuminating the blue waters, which became pale and nacreous under the caress of the luminous effluvia.

As a light wind stirred the foliage, it sometimes seemed that white phantoms were passing beneath the crowns, and the floating vapors that were running over the murmurous waves appeared by turns to be swans with quivering plumage, or pisciform naiads. Also conquered by the charm of the hour, I did not say anything, and it was Justus who broke the silence.

"I've never accepted," he said, "the legend that announced the death of Pan. Assuredly, my friend, the gods aren't dead."

"I'd like to believe you," I sighed, "and it would please me to imagine that Hermes, fatigued by his incessant voyages, might come to sit at our table and ask for a glass of beer to wash down some of those little gingery sausages you like so much."

"You're incredulous," the counselor replied, "and you aren't truly worthy of attracting the attention of the Olympians. On evenings like this, it wouldn't astonish me at all to find Apollo sitting on my doorstep, going among the shepherds again."

"You think it's sufficient to believe, then?" I asked him.

"I'm sure of it," he replied, "and I knew a believer who lived for years in the company of an immortal."

"Tell me about that, my good Justus," I exclaimed.

"Gladly," he replied, "even though you're a miscreant."

He took a long swig, relit his pipe, and started to narrate, as Hoffmann's heroes narrate.

All the inhabitants of this region have retained in their minds the name and the memory of Heinrich von Helneim, for that young gentleman, during the years that he wanted to consecrate to the world, showed himself to be the most benevolent, most tender and best of men. He was scarcely out of university when he became an orphan, and having felt an extreme pain in the loss of his parents, he set forth, in order to distract himself, to travel through Europe. Rich and good-looking, with a slightly frail and effeminate but seductive beauty, everywhere he went he was able to know and savor all pleasures, the basest and the most refined, those one can buy and those that are dispensed to the privileged of the society of fortune and birth. Simultaneously sentimental and sensual, passionate and a dreamer, he was born to love and to suffer from loving; of an excessive sensibility, he had a tendency to hypochondria, a tendency that he got from his mother, a pale Scotswoman, slim and red-haired with eyes forever veiled with tears, who died abruptly one evening, bent over the ground, as lilies die.

Those who frequented Heinrich in his youth remembered him as a rather morose, taciturn companion, refusing obstinately to deliver himself, but in spite of that, sociable, welcoming and generous. During his travels he did not cultivate amity for anyone, but it appears certain that he loved. Whom did he love? How was his amour engaged and disengaged? No one ever knew. In order to talk about the object of his passion he would have had to vanquish a naïve and incurable timidity; however, we have always been reduced here to conjectures, for Heinrich von Helneim did not favor us with his confidences when he returned to live in the country of his birth, not to quit it again.

During the first weeks of his sojourn, he was often encountered in the streets of the city, and it was noticeable that he had grown considerably thinner, and that the expression of sadness that customarily impregnated his features was aggravated. He took long solitary walks, distractedly returning the salutes of those who inclined in going past him, but scarcely responding with curt and dry remarks to the indiscreet individuals who went so far as to solicit his conversation.

Soon, the curiosity that surrounded him seemed to embarrass him; he spaced out his excursions, and when one encountered him among the cherry-trees of steep paths, he turned away to avoid gazes. A day came when he was no longer seen. He occupied a vast house situated in the middle of an immense garden in the heights of the town, and he lived there with a few old and faithful family servants. All that anyone knew later of his existence, after the tragic denouement that concluded it, was learned from his butler, Otto, an old man who had seen him born and who died of his death.

When he had closed the doors of his dwelling, not to open them again, a singular preoccupation seemed to invade him. On the walls of the large rooms hung a rich and precious collection of paintings by the most famous masters of the eighteenth century, accumulated by an ancestor smitten with that genteel, seductive and charming art. Heinrich had all the canvases and pastels removed in which the painters had represented the women of times past, in languid poses, with touching grace, painted with the attributes of goddesses or shepherdesses as adornment. The bright smiles of those nymphs, illuminating the panels of violet-tinted wood, irritated and obsessed him, and he only found respite when he was solely in the company of booted and spurred gentlemen costumed for hunting or for war.

From then on he spent all his days shut away in a drawing room on the ground floor, into which he had had his bed transported. A perpetual night reigned in that room, where he slept and took his meals. When evening came, once the stars were illuminated in the firmament, he quit that retreat, went down into the park, and wandered through the pathways until morning.

Impelled by the same sentiments, he had ordered that all the statues that ornamented the clumps of bushes and the lawns be taken down, and he had relegated the images of Venus, Ceres and Pomona to the cellars. He had only respected a Diana with muscular legs and slender, hard arms, chastely enveloped by the abundant pleats of her short and high-necked tunic. It was in her company that he came to seek nocturnal repose. He stayed for long hours, his forehead applied to the feet of the huntress, murmuring vague words that the wind carried away.

On moonlit nights he seemed more agitated, and a sort of delirium took possession of him. The pedestal of the goddess was near the water of a small tranquil lake, and her virginal forms were reflected in the polished mirror of its surface. Then, Heinrich bent over the bright sheet, in which the form that appeared to him seemed more immaterial and more virginal, and he often raised his eyes to the heavens, to contemplate the cold star, and, looking at the statue again, he compared its pallor to the sororal pallor of the Moon.

Then he withdrew, pursuing the brilliant rays through the thickets, as if he wanted to follow the immortal into the green forest. He rendered a worship to it, and gradually, he animated it; amid the enclosed lawns and the hornbeam hedges he heard the barking of dogs, and he lay in wait in the middle of clearings for the emergence from cover of a pursued deer.

One evening, his servants saw him go down the marble perron in an outdated costume. He was wearing a white chlamys; he had ringed his head with scabious and, as he marched, he was talking in a rhythmic fashion. Otto followed him to the foot of the altar that he had erected before the beloved effigy and heard him say:

"I, whom Aphrodite has deceived, have come to you as young Hippolytus once came, O dearest of goddesses, daughter of Leto, and I address to you the prayer that the son of Theseus addressed to you: 'Salutation, O very beautiful, most beautiful of the virgins that inhabit Olympus, Artemis! O mistress, I give you this crown woven in an untrodden meadow, which iron has never touched, where no pastor has dared to graze his flock, where only the bees of spring come and modesty fecundates with its dew. O dear mistress, receive therefore from my pious hands this crown for your gilded hair. In fact, to me alone among mortals this gift has been accorded, that I accompany you, speak to you and hear your voice.'"

After having spoken thus, Heinrich covered Diana's breast with his flowers, and, embracing the knees of the divinity, wept copiously. Trembling with terror, Otto hid behind a juniper bush, and was about to flee when, wiping his moist face, Helneim went on:

"But Hippolytus had always been faithful to you, goddess, and I have failed your laws. Rancor, despair and sorrow have not expiated my crime; one last sacrifice is necessary to you, and it is at your feet that I shall accomplish it."

There was a silence, and Otto recounts that he saw the face of the Olympian lean over Heinrich. Then he heard a terrible scream: a scream of horror. He ran forward, and received his master in his arms.

The unfortunate had mutilated himself abominably; he was losing his blood through a frightful wound, and, as he refused all help, deaf to supplications and to tears, he expired the following day, after a gentle agony.

"Thus died Heinrich von Helneim," Justus concluded, "for whom Artemis the huntress descended from Olympus once again."

"Your Heinrich was a madman, Justus," I said to him.

"That's possible," he replied. "Nevertheless, he knew the amour of a goddess. Who wouldn't want to be mad and to perish, at that price?"

The Merchant of Silence

"ISN'T this the land of the fays?" asked Nalle.
It was evening, and from the room in which dinner was being served, hills could be seen scaled by vines, and the soft, pale girdle with which the river circled the meadows. The guests were numerous, they were cheerful, and the roast had just been served when Nalle posed his question.

"Isn't this the land of the fays?"

"Yes," Anselme replied; "this is where they lived before their exile. They amused themselves in the middle of those lawns, for they were coquettish, like women, and loved to be seen. They only hid behind tree-trunks when men who were too ugly came toward them, and legend reports that they only acted thus to spare those wretches dolor, whose souls were ulcerated by the sight of beauty. They lived on the edges of pools and mirrored themselves herein when dusk fell; they were hospitable and gentle, and it was them who led the Celts, lovers of water, to the springs."

"You speak of them as if you believed in them," interjected Claude.

"Why shouldn't I believe in them? If I've often dreamed about them, they must necessarily exist."

Everyone started laughing, and Anselme was obliged to submit to a few gibes and sarcasms. He took no notice, and went on:

"First of all, I believe in everything as a poet, although I believe in very few as a philosopher. To distract and recreate my mind, I amuse myself sometimes by delivering myself to chimeras. On certain propitious evenings, like this one, I believe in revenants as I believe in virtue, I believe in spirits as I believe in the stupidity and ignominy of humans, I believe in sylphs, goblins, genies, kobolds, salamanders, elves, roussalkas, lorelei, lavandières and korrigans; I believe in apparitions—which is to say, the unexplained, if not the inexplicable."

"To believe in all that, it's necessary to have seen," said Claude.

"How do you know," retorted Anselme, "that I haven't witnessed some mysterious scene capable of reawakening infantile beliefs in me, to which, by virtue of the desire for repose, by virtue of melancholy laziness, I was able lend myself for a few moments?"

"Oh, tell us about that, Anselme," someone exclaimed. "Tell us about that!"

"Gladly. It's a strange story, but from which you might obtain profit. Perhaps you'll be incredulous, you'll accuse me of being hallucinated and a visionary. I'll respond to you in advance that I wasn't the only witness to the adventure; I certainly can't be the only one to remember it, for it left too grave and too profound an emotion in the minds of those who were mixed up in it, and it's difficult to invoke a collective hallucination."

He leaned his elbows on the table, supporting his head in his lands; furrowing his brow, he seemed to be recalling obscure details from the depths of his memory, and after a few minutes of a silence that the witnesses respected, he told the tale.

You still remember, I imagine, the banker Silben. The ten years that have gone by since his death can't have made you forget the man whose gold dominated Paris. He was an incomparable rogue, a condottiere of finance, a strategist of the Bourse, who carried out his speculations as Napoléon did his campaigns, pillaging millions as conquerors pillage provinces.

No one knew where he came from; some said England, others Germany; some asserted that he was French, and originally from the Auvergne, others preferred Belgium. Personally, I believe that he had no homeland; he was universal, like a symbol, and had doubtless chosen Paris for his territory because Paris is a cosmopolitan center. His depredations were legendary; like triumphant generals, he was surrounded by ruins, and his glory was made of the misery and death of human beings. So he was respected, and had, it was said, neither dread nor remorse.

He was very learned; he adored the arts and loved letters; he was not attached to the gold he conquered; he was generous, even prodigal; it was said that after having ruined a rival financier, he enriched him, only wanting the honor of having defeated him. He invited all Paris to countless fêtes, but he never attended his parties, his feasts and his balls, only amusing himself in the society of a few people that he was accustomed to receive in a modest country house on the edge of the Oise, where he forgot that he was rich.

Silben was tall, strong and very handsome; he inspired passions in women who were unaware of his fortune. No man ever gave me the impression as much as him of perfect intellectual and physical health. However, you all know that Silben died in an asylum, raving mad, restrained in a straitjacket, howling under cold showers and beatings. Perhaps I was the only one, in the times of his splendor, who divined and foresaw his end. How? That is connected to the singular event about which I want to talk to you.

"I was closely linked with Silben. He interested me, as a beautiful bird of prey can be interesting, or a wild beast without scruple or regard. He liked me because I made it a rule not to ask him for any service and we could speak freely about people and things. So, I was a familiar of Aiguelande, which was the name of his villa; I often spent entire weeks there, and in 1887, to flee the noise of Paris, I was taking refuge there.

"At Aiguelande there were a dozen of us, all men, for Silben proscribed women from his retreat. You'll understand why I'm not giving the names of the other guests. Know, however, that among them there was a soldier whose ferocity during the civil wars had rendered him celebrated; a novelist devoid of a conscience, who owed his renown to the most shameless plagiarisms and the most abominable base actions; an illustrious philosopher whose entire existence had been employed in panegyrics to force and injustice; a physician and a chemist whose peccadilloes were no longer counted; and two financiers, regular agents of Silben's, hardened to all tasks, armored against all tears and also against all insults.

It was a day in June, an evening like this one, when the moonlight was laminating the surface of the Oise with silver, an evening of tranquility and peace. We were at table; the last service had just been cleared away, the coffee and liqueurs had been served, the domestics—who were not very numerous in any case—had withdrawn, and we were chatting.

It was the philosopher who had the floor. With his specious artistry and his subtle skill he was talking about great criminals, analyzing their insensibility in a marvelous and clear fashion. Expanding his subject, he talked about remorse, seeing it as proof of a psychic inferiority, attributing it to sensory reflexes, the ideological reaction to violent impressions, which only the unbalanced could feel.

When he had finished, no one replied to him. One might have thought that a shadow of inexplicable melancholy had suddenly extended over the brow of those men. Silben was mechanically making breadcrumbs, the novelist was drumming his fingers on the table, while the chemist was dipping the butt of his cigar in the brandy that filled his glass; and the silence was threatening to endure when I saw the door open and a man appear on the threshold.

He was not an habitué of Aiguelande; I had never seen him there before, nor in the neighborhood, which I knew quite well. Although he was dressed in a somewhat worn frock-coat with long tails, and was carrying a canvas sack slung over his shoulder, he did not look like a vagabond. His features did not lack nobility; he had a high forehead and sad blue eyes, and in spite of the abundance of a graying beard, one divined that his mouth was creased and dolorous.

Although he was shod in strong boots he was walking soundlessly; his cane was balanced softly on the floor, and he advanced like that into the middle of the room. There he stopped, scanning the guests—whom having finally perceived him were examining him with surprise—with a saddened gaze, and he remained silent and motionless until Silben had asked him in a voice whose anxiety was poorly dissimulated by its rudeness: "Where have you come from? Who are you?"

Then the unknown man approached the table and, placing his hands on the philosopher's chair, he said, slowly: "I am the Merchant of Silence."

I saw the hands of all those surrounding me clench on the tablecloth, and the soldier, with a convulsive movement, broke his glass, stained the linen with a few crimson droplets. A strange stupor dilated their pupils, but no one replied.

The old man tapped his sack then, and said: "I have it here, and I sell it. Speak, and I shall open the sack, and I'll give you what you want: Silence. Be generous, and for you, I shall make the rumors that assail your ears shut up, and the clamors that you repel in vain. You are not unaware of the stridency of anger, the poignant sound of sobs, the murmur of softly proffered plaints, the precipitate or suppliant repetition of prayers; I can appease all those that pursue you, and the voices of which importune you, even though you disdain them. I shall kill the sound for you, I shall prepare the realm of peace for you and calm will descend within you, to such an extent . . . to such an extent that you will no longer hear anything but your own interior voices: you will hear yourselves. Don't let me go away; I won't come back here again—and know this: few men have been able, like you, to encounter the Merchant of Silence."

All of them—the soldier and the philosopher, the novelist and the physician, the chemist and the financiers—got up then and went out, their faces convulsed by the most abject terror.

Silben and I stayed, and, the stranger having made a sign, Silben stood up in his turn, and followed him. I remained dazed momentarily, and then, having seen them both disappear, I hurled myself in pursuit of them through the corridors; but the old man had disappeared, and I only found Silben at the bottom of the garden, collapsed on a bench.

I called to him; he raised his head, and put a finger over his mouth. "Shh!" he said. "I'm the only one to have bought the Silence. I'm beginning to hear my own voice."

Anselme stopped.

"Can you conceive that at certain times, I can believe in the inexplicable?" he asked. "Certainly, I believe in it, and on this similar summer evening, in this similar moonlight, beside this table, I seem to hear behind the closed door the footsteps of the Merchant of Silence."

Very pale, the gusts turned toward the door, but it remained closed, and no one saw the Merchant of Silence come in.

The Eternal Wait

ASSUREDLY, not all those who were gathered in Anselme's house that Christmas Eve were celebrating the nativity in their hearts. Nevertheless, without being believers, those men were religious, because they admired and loved beautiful ideologies, harmonious myths and touching legends. They were familiar with metaphysics and with symbols, and if they did not accord to them the absolute faith that they were accustomed to give to science, they animated them and considered them as living, since they had been powerful generators of ideas and images.

So, after the meal that had been the pretext for their gathering, they did not converse about futile subjects. They thought, involuntarily, that in these times, still so obscure, midnight was one of the rare moments capable of evoking in simple souls sentiments that depress quotidian life. To all those whom the essential systems, the search for the truth and its pursuit, left insensible, that midnight brought unusual and fortunate preoccupations; it exalted their being and thus rendered them more accessible, no doubt, to the scattered beauty and bounty that they could not conceive without intermediaries, without incarnating them in legends, dogmas or superstitions. So they talked about all that and, at the same time, the reanimated in their memory the thoughts and visions of old.

"Believe me," said Nalle, "we're more attached to the past than we commonly believe. In our young brains and our credulous hearts, beliefs have been deposited on our entry into life that we cannot succeed, alas, in killing by means of reflection. Phantoms dwell within us, of which, without taking account of it, we maintain the life, and they often guide us, push us and drag us; they emerge from the unconscious and appear to our astonished eyes. We regard them at first as strangers, intruders who disturb our conceptions, but we don't take long to recognize them, and we take pleasure in allowing ourselves to be lulled and deceived by them."

"That's true," said Anselme, "and those phantoms do even more. They're capable of engendering new forms in us; they combine with our present ideas, they influence our concepts, they denature them and make us see them from unexpected angles, under strange aspects."

"Oh," Claude interrupted, "you're complicated, Anselme, and you, Nalle. I, who, like you, am not a Christian, but a simple man, believe again in Jesus once a year, only I don't believe as I did in the times when I stammered prayers. When Christmas comes around, I don't prostrate myself before an altar, but it seems to me that the Galilean, the good prophet who vagabonded over the shores of lakes, is really going to be born again and bring something new into the world, as he did once before, it's said, when people were, as they still are, tormented and anxious. Every year, when the twelve solemn chimes ring out, I think about the chagrin and anguish of the poor, the sufferings and the iniquities, and I wait for the justice of Jesus, which is going to be reborn."

"You're not the only one, my dear Claude," said Anselme. "There are others haunted by the same childish dream: fervent adherents of the Millennium, believers in the Golden Age and the reign of God, which, if ever it is realized, will be the reign of evil on earth. That faith of the Millenarians is not only fantastic or sporadic, like yours, Claude, it's often a sectarian faith; it dresses in the strangest forms, and our discussion reminds me of a singular adventure of the explorer Mailler. I'll tell you about it if you like, such as it was told to me on an evening like this one. Close your eyes, don't see Anselme any longer, and imagine that it's the illustrious voyager who's speaking to you."

※

It was six years ago, after a long voyage in Asia, over the high plateaux; I was returning to Europe. In the month of July, after several days of overwhelming heat, I was obliged to stop *en route*, in the middle of one of the least known valleys of the Liban, in a village whose name I have never seen on any map: a peaceful village of a thousand inhabitants, the constructions of which were backed up to the Snowy Mountain.

Laid low by malady and fatigue, I stayed there for two weeks in a small house sheltered by oaks and wild pistachio bushes. After the first few days of fever I was able to get up and, although I was still weak, to mingle with the life of the people who had taken me in. I took advantage of that to study them and question them.

The village had only been built ten years before. The people who had founded it had settled in that solitude not only in order to be far away from the world, but also to live in a place that was, in their eyes, sanctified, for, when they quit their dwellings and climbed the steep slopes, they could contemplate the peaks of Horeb, Tabor and Carmel, and in the distance they could see the Mountain of Blessings, the one that, according to legend, heard the prophet of Nazareth speaking to his humble flock.

The inhabitants of the valley had fled the cities that they found too tumultuous and too sinful; they had come to seek peace and future happiness. They had all belonged to the class of the petty people, the host of partisans who sweat and toil for their daily bread, bent over the daily task, quitting the hard labor at nightfall and resuming it at dawn, with no other horizon than the establishment or the work over which they were curbed, ignorant of immediate joys, only sustained on the long and harsh route by the vague hope of possible felicities.

They had been taken there by one of the apostles that emerge so frequently in that part of Asia Minor, whom the blood of the first martyrs seems to have impregnated with fervor. The word of that man had had no difficulty taking them away from their labor and had brought into bloom all the flowers of hope that were germinating in their hearts. They had marched behind him, happy and enthusiastic, and they now lived, huddled like sheep around a shepherd, with the man who had taken them away from the world, to dolor and obedience.

Thus my host had spoken to me, and I was burning with desire to see the man who had acquired such an influence on him and his companions, when he came into the house one morning. He was an extremely thin old man with a white and bushy beard, a forehead that was high and, extraordinarily, as smooth as that of an infant. He had large bright eyes that were sometimes drowned by a mist of tears, a hooked and willful nose dividing a face that, without that eagle's beak, would have seemed slack and irresolute, and hair that was still black and curly, falling over his shoulders, contrasting strangely with the pale flood of his beard.

He was clad in a long robe of smooth brown wool, gathered at the waist by a rope. In spite of the sun's ardor, no hat covered his head, and he walked barefoot, leaning on a staff of olive-wood. He bowed before me and wished me welcome. As I had stood up in order to receive him, he made me a sign to sit down, and taking his place by my side, he interrogated me.

"Have you come to stay among us?"

"No," I replied. "I'm like the passer-by who stops by a stream in order to drink, wash his feet crippled by lassitude and gather new strength, in order to depart again in the sunlight."

I spoke to him in that imagistic language because I knew that his soul was candid and more open to parables than to reasoning. He reflected after listening to me.

"Since you have savored repose for an hour," he said, "how can you resume your route, going toward fatigues, disappointments and dangers? Here you would only have peace, and, which is inestimable, liberty. For days, months and years I traveled the cities. I preached to those I encountered disobedience to the laws of men and respect for the divine laws that are not always written. I have awakened their minds from heavy slumber; I have confronted them with themselves, I have taught them to know themselves, to break the chains with which they had been charged since the day of their birth, and all those to whom slavery was odious have come with me."

"Perhaps you are right," I replied, "and it is doubtless vanity that prevents me from remaining with you in this valley unknown to men, embalmed by aromatic plants and perfumed by the memory of a God. But I believe that I too have a mission to fulfill and actions that solicit me—and what would I do here?"

"You would do as we do; you would wait."

"What would I wait for?"

Then the old man drew closer to me. He lowered his voice and said: "You would wait for the coming of the Lord, the new Noël. It is because I knew that the time was near that I brought these people here. The earth is overburdened with misery, the scourges of justice, authority and human cruelty have ravaged the soil, they have strewn debris and ruins, and Jesus cannot be long delayed in surging forth to save his faithful. One night, when unknown stars will shine in the heavens, he will appear again to some. That is why we are waiting here, near the hills that were familiar to him, and he would already have come to visit us if it were not for the Jew."

"The Jew?" I queried. "What Jew?"

The apostle hesitated momentarily, as if he dared not confide in me, and then he decided to tell me about the lamentable adventure.

One day, a sordid vagabond had arrived in the village. Bowed down, his features withered, his eyes dull and his head bare, he seemed to be carrying on his back the weight of thousands of years. He was bloodied by the bushes of the roadside; he was dragging himself along with difficulty, and he collapsed in front of the first house.

He was taken in. His wounds were bandaged, he was given garments, and slowly, he seemed to be reborn. When a few weeks had gone by, the prophet interrogated him, asking him whether he wanted to pray with them for the imminent coming of the Lord.

To that request, the wanderer replied that he would like to remain in that corner of mildness and peace, but that he could not consent to mingle his voice with those of others, for he had neither the same faith nor the same desires. He asked that he be allowed to dwell there in that haven for which he had not hoped, where he would wait for a benevolent and liberating death. When the other hesitated, he declared that, having assisted in the execution of the Christ, he was unable to request his return.

After that declaration, a great stupor invaded the village; a council was held, and then the most persuasive men were sent to the visitor who was polluting the air in order to enjoin him not to trouble any longer the repose of those who had not summoned him. It was in vain and, doubtless to avenge himself on them, the

Jew gathered them all together at dusk and harangued them.

"Men, you believe yourselves to be just, you think you are in possession of the truth, and your pride is such that you cannot accept among you someone who does not accept your dogmas. You speak in the name of liberty but your most natural effort is to exercise constraint. You have only escaped violence to practice it yourselves; you have not understood that everyone, according to his own strength, marches toward the goal that he has chosen. Because of that criminal forgetfulness, you are not worthy of that for which you are hoping, and you must be punished.

"Do you not know the prophecies? I am the eternal Jew, the one who, wanting no master, did not bow down under the blood of the cross and would not accept your chains. Do you not know that Jesus will only return on the day when I shall recognize him? If he has made me carry a heavy and centuries-old burden, he is nevertheless charged with my bonds; it is my will alone that can make him descend from the heaven where you have placed him and where I oblige him to remain. When my stiff neck flexes before him, when my proud forehead touches his feet, then he will be free and can return among you. But the hour has not come, and, because you have rejected me, my unique power will break yours."

In repeating those terrible words the old man was sobbing recklessly. Gripped by a secret curiosity, I asked him to take me to that Ahasuerus. He acceded to my request and took me to a crude hut, in the depths of which I saw the man who was the vagabond. We stopped on the threshold, for, with a curt gesture the Jew forbade us to enter, and I heard his hoarse voice say:

"He will come when I wish it."

"We are waiting for him even so," the prophet said to me, "and he will one day cry after him."

Oh, I thought, *may your wish not be granted! Such as he is, how necessary that Jew is to your poor souls! Is it not him alone who can support your desires, enable your foolish hope to live? And how precious that ironic solitary is to your dreams, which, but for him, insensible time would wound mortally.*

The same evening, I quit the valley, never to return. And the memory of that sad apostle was effaced from my mind, and I forgot him, as I forgot the man in whom I thought to see the Wandering Jew.

"That," concluded Anselme, "was what Mailler told me one Christmas Eve, and I shared his opinion: that the illusion of the wait was the auxiliary chimera of those wretches, that it was indispensable to them, that it enabled them to conceive the possible and realizable happiness. But when I thought about that bizarre adventure later, I started to desire ardently the day when the phantoms that deceive thirst, hunger and need will no longer be necessary to humans, because humans will no longer be suffering."

Forgetfulness

"HALF of our life is made of memories, and the actions we carry out every day only acquire their full value when we compare them to the actions of the past. It is thanks to those abolished things, which are nevertheless still living, that we savor temporary accidents. Our memory is populated by phantoms, and we can evoke them at our will; they haunt us and assail us, they animate our most secret solitudes, and our existence is tricked out by them like a magical theater whose scenery and apparatus we can vary incessantly. In the foreground, present events appear; they are the actors in the play, those one sees first; but from the depths of perspective it is given to us to bring forth at our appeal the pale shades of old, which advance in processions, placing themselves in the manner of antique choruses, then draw away and are lost again in the distance, while we sense their presence confusedly behind the canvas and the supportive frames.

"There are some, however, who do not know those joys; there are people whose minds are like a dull mirror incapable of reflection; they are the unfortunates who only grasp the passing moment and are deprived of the tender and faithful companions of yore. In the memory the images sink like stones thrown into the depths of leaden lakes; they know that they have penetrated the dismal and echoless surface, but they cannot resuscitate them and make them laugh or weep before them, and for those sad living people, the past is nothing but a vast necropolis inhabited by names and signs, not forms."

Having said that, Anselme stood up; he opened a heavy walnut dresser, which was the principal ornament of his study; he took out of one of the drawers a slender scroll of paper and came back toward us.

"I knew one of the men of which I was speaking, and you know him too; he was one of your friends—or, at least, you liked him, even though he was silent, and never confided to anyone his chagrins, his dolors, or the long and terrible torture he endured for many years. Which of you does not remember Henri Daville? He was, as you know, a subtle and profound metaphysician, one of those familiars of the absolute, whose spirit moved in the midst of abstract and symbolic essences more easily than through the phenomena of the visible universe. The work that he left, *On the Real Life of Ideas and their Transitory Reflection*, has permitted all of you, in any case, to penetrate his personality.

"You have doubtless not forgotten Daville's death, and if I recall it, it is to comment on what it remains for me to tell you. He lived in the depths of Vaugirard in a little student room only furnished with a bed, a chair and a table, with a white wood shelf unit on the wall filled with books. No engravings, no trinkets— nothing that could indicate any attachment whatsoever to exterior life. He never went out, except to come here—which is to say, three times a week—and for one hour every morning, which he spent walking along the fortifications, taking the same route every day, in order, so he said, to expend a constant sum of energy. No one knew whether he had parents, or any affections other than the amicable ones with which he favored us.

"One morning, the daily woman who took care of his humble household went into his room, to which she had a duplicate key, and found Daville dead in his bed. He had killed himself with a revolver shot to the heart. Panicking, she shouted for help, the neighbors came running and, as they found a large envelope on the table with my name on it, one of them came to fetch me.

"I shall never forget the spectacle that was offered to me. In order to die, Daville had lain down on a carpet of flowers. His body was disappearing under a flood of anemones and buttercups, his grave face aureoled by yellowing roses, and the hand that had held the weapon had fallen back in the fresh corollas. That philosopher, whom we supposed to be insensible to the powerful charm of things, had agonized in the midst of joy, colors and perfumes.

"Few of us, you will remember, followed Daville's convoy. He was then unknown to everyone except a few official professors who developed his theories in heavy tracts, avoiding naming their inspirer, and only benevolent death was able to give the philosopher the posthumous glory that is increasing every day. At that sad moment, the admirers and friends of the man who is now the master of a young multitude were the five of us, who had learned to know and love him for a long time.

"What were our conjectures, that day, to explain that unexpected death, that abrupt and impenetrable suicide? Because you were all ignorant, as I was, of Daville's intimate life, your suppositions were numerous and vain, and it was only on the evening of the burial that the veil was torn away for me when I opened the bequeathed envelope.

"It contained, along with the two essays, which I published, on *The Possible Realization of Ideas*, these few pages of confidences. I have not communicated them to you sooner because it was necessary for me to conform to Daville's formal instruction. He had asked me to keep this missive secret for two years, in order, he said, for you to be able to judge it more freely, and I have chosen the anniversary of his death to read these brief notes to you."

Everyone drew nearer to Anselme, and he read Daville's letter.

⁂

My dear friend, the confidence that you have always testified to me and the amity that you have devoted, not merely to my person but also to my ideas, give me an obligation to converse with you during the last hours that remain for me to live. That obligation is pleasant for me; I experience a kind of tranquil joy in making my confession to you, in thus examining the depths of my being one last time and showing you all that there has been of human sadness in an existence that you thought dedicated uniquely to the cult of pure essences and the absolute.

In any case, even if those sentiments did not exist in me, you would have the right to ask me for an explanation, since I have mingled my life slightly with yours, and I cannot quit you so abruptly without a word of adieu. Suppose, then, my dear friend, that I am writing to you after a visit, to excuse myself for not coming back.

I have not told you anything about my life and you are ignorant of my origins, my childhood, my education, my adolescence and my maturity prior to the day when I encountered you. Forgive me for that silence, and forgive me also for not breaking it even now, and see no cause for it except an invincible modesty. The infantile wails of my spirit cannot matter to you, can they, since you have known me as a man, and what value would there be in the story of my first tentative steps on the way to what I have believed, and still believe, to be the truth?

I have appeared to you as a cold and melancholy soul, a metaphysician whom only infinity could seduce, a poor being whom worldly joys left indifferent. You were both right and wrong. I was sad and taciturn, one of those men whose heart is closed by a triple seal; nevertheless, I was not as insensible as you might have believed to certain passions. For a long time, I was closed to everything that was not my thought, but on the day when I was conquered, I was overcome forever.

I have loved, with a profound and violent amour, if not with my senses, at least with my spirit. Do not ask me anything about the person who opened my eyes and my heart; I do not want to say anything about her, for it would be insupportable that, with me dead, others could represent to themselves the dear image that I have been unable to keep. As to where I met her, how she conquered me, what our existence was, allow me to remain silent, and don't conserve any sentiment in consequence. Only know that for two years, I savored the plenitude of happiness.

After two unforgettable years, my wife—for she had become my wife—died. Again I found myself alone, alone with the memory of past hours, and it was then that the abominable torture commenced for me. Of the person who had fled, I had retained nothing that could remind me of her. I had put everything into the coffin that had been taken away, dressing the dead woman in her only robe, ornamenting her with the few jewels that she had loved, and not even her image remained to me, for I had never wanted to see fixed on paper or canvas the person whose living presence I always had by my side.

For some time I continued to occupy the small apartment where she had lived with me; I only abandoned it when the house was demolished to make way for new streets; then I came to live in the small room where you have always known me, and which became for me more terrible than the most terrible of the circles of the Florentine's Inferno.

Nothing around me recalled henceforth the memory of my beloved, and, deprived of the customary auxiliaries, my increasingly recalcitrant memory refused to evoke her. Living and present beside me during the first days of the separation, I saw her visage slowly pale; she seemed to retreat into a realm of dreams, clad in mists that thickened over her features by the hour, and sometimes she fled my voice to the extent that I could scarcely distinguish her, hiding in the midst of the fog that invaded my poor mind.

Soon, it was only at the expense of great efforts that I succeeded in representing her to myself, and the moment came when any evocation became impossible for me. I closed my eyes and extended my will in vain; I could no longer see anything but a long, frail, veiled form. But that form still spoke, and its voice was the cherished voice, the caressant voice that came from the shadows to put my anguish to sleep again.

However, even the voice was to fade; I sensed it slowing down, becoming heavy, dying away into a vague and troubling murmur, from which a familiar word something burst forth. Then, that adored sound fell silent in the eddies of a uniform and monotonous mutter into which the voice that still gave me the illusion of life eventually sank.

All my efforts were impotent to reconquer the lost vision, and I lived abominable years, softly murmuring the beloved name that I do not even want to tell you: years of torture, in which all memory fled me, until, today, I can no longer bear to live in the dark well, devoid of visions and echoes, that is my life.

I have just bought the flowers that she preferred; that is the only means that I still have of stimulating my memory, with a perfume and colors that she loved. I have often surrounded myself thus with roses and anemones. I once hoped that the image of the dead woman would come to play in the midst of what she had cherished; now that I can no longer believe it, I am weary of struggling against myself, and now that you have been my confessor, nothing more remains for me but to die.

If you ask me why I am dying, I will reply to you that it is truly to conquer forgetfulness, the forgetfulness that has been my torturer and will be my benevolent healer. You will doubtless criticize my resolution, and perhaps you will be right, but that decisive night is necessary to my mind and my heart. I am a philosopher but I am not a Stoic, nor, alas, a hero; it is therefore necessary that I disappear, that I quit a life that I can no longer live.

Adieu, then, my dear friend. I have consigned separately a few desires that I would like you to accomplish, and a few indications relative to the manuscript that I am confiding to you. I thank you, for you will observe my wishes; thank you also for having listened to me. You, whose reason is so clear and so valiant, will grant me a little indulgent and tender pity.

Anselme fell silent, while his listeners meditated silently.

Pity

ON the edge of the Atlantic Ocean, within the confines of Brittany, I am making the confession of this adventure. It is so sweetly sorrowful that I rejoice in being confessed near rigid cliffs, in this somewhat bleak but grandiose location, where the melancholy voice of the sea lends an elevated and noble gravity to spoken words.

We were, in this lost burg, a little colony of painters, litterateurs and philosophers, and the phalanstery that we formed was sagely regulated. By day, each of us followed his instincts and inclinations freely, but we had adopted the custom of gathering after the evening meal to exchange our impressions and ideas in a familiar fashion.

It was, therefore, evening, at the placid hour that precedes the night, when the waves take off their sparkling robe in order to envelop themselves in a taciturn mantle, when the murmur of the swell inflates, filling the air with a poignant harmony and indecisive perfumes coming from mysterious lands, unknown and veiled isles, agitate and float in the atmosphere. We had already been talking for some time, and it would be difficult for me to reconstitute the beginnings of the conversation, when Nalle, addressing the metaphysician Marc, extending his hand toward the strand, exclaimed:

"Ought I to confess to you, my friend the philosopher, that it does not displease me to see on this beach those dirty and rickety children, and those women reminiscent of female animals lying in wait for their prey. They are in harmony with the landscape, with these bare rocks, these arid sands, that meager gorse, and even the pity that they inspire in me enables me to savor the spectacle of nature more fully, as our master Rousseau might have said."

"That confession does not diminish you in my eyes," Marc replied. "You are similar in that to the majority of men, and it even seems to me that you do not insist forcefully enough on the correlation that exists between your pity and your joy."

"What! You think so?" interrogated Nalle.

"I believe, my friend, that the greatest pleasure that a man can experience is feeling compassion for someone—which is to say, measuring his strength by the other's weakness. The exercise of pity permits pride and human egotism to arrive at their highest degree of exaltation, and thus procures the most agreeable sensations."

"You can't think that," interjected the poet Alain.

"I think," Marc affirmed, "that the best of us has experienced, in exercising pity, a purely egoistical satisfaction, simply by comparing himself to those who render him compassionate, in sensing a slight but sharp and terrifying frisson at the idea that he might one day find himself in the same state as those to whom he has just accorded his pity. Don't you agree, Anselme?"

"You're right, Marc, and I'll recount to you one of the brief and transitory adventures that might serve to support your thesis."

"Speak."

You have all, for an hour, and perhaps for years of your life, loved the night, and I have not escaped the common law. Ten years ago, I cherished that marvelous auxiliary of dreams, and I was, as Nalle ought to remember, one of the most renowned night-owls in Paris. We often vagabonded until dawn together. But I ought to say that, in spite of the amity that linked me, and still links me, to Nalle, I had always preferred to be alone in my nocturnal excursions. In the night I was seeking an unknown, which, it seemed to me, would only reveal itself to a solitary, and the importunate sound of the dialogues dear to peripatetic couples, chases away the visions that take pleasure in silence.

So, without a companion, I roamed around darkened Paris, amusing myself in the deserted back streets that, under the twisted flames of gas-lamps, were populated by faint forms, and I followed the phantasmal army of my desires through remote, distant and obscure places. Sometimes, I stopped for long hours at the railings of a house a long way out, toward Passy, and mechanically, awaited the one who was to come, thinking invincibly about the young woman who emerged by night to console and love the Opium-Eater.

One winter morning, I was going back to my lodgings, at the disquieting hour when night and dawn are disputing the heavens, when the dear shadows are drawing away that leave regret in souls of not having attained them, at the same time as the pleasure of having pursued them vanishes. I was walking with a heavy and trailing tread, for I was exhausted by my excursion, which had been longer than usual; I was going mechanically, semi-somnolent, my eyes almost closed, as if to shut out the nascent daylight, and I do not know where my quasi-somnambulistic march might have taken me if I had not suddenly sensed on my shoulder the contact, as light as the flutter of a wing, of a hand that descended gently upon me.

I shivered, my eyelids lifted, I recognized my door, and I was about to ring, without thinking any more about the incident that had roused me from my torpor, the memory of which had fled with the awakening, when I heard my name pronounced by an exceedingly slow and weary voice.

I turned round abruptly; I saw a woman behind me, and I remembered that her fingers had touched me. I looked at her for a long time. She was young, even very young; that was visible in the candor of her eyes, of a placid watery green, communicating to her face the impression of adolescent tenderness given by little lakes in the clearings of woods. Her emaciated face was devoid of wrinkles; it had a mat pallor that rendered even more gripping the ribbon of red lips; it was dominated by a smooth and slightly prominent forehead and tapered in a long, narrow chin: a face that would have been hieratic and glacial but for the straight, slightly flesh nose, which put life into that mask of a wise virgin whom foolish virgins had led astray.

As she had called me by name, I searched in the lines of her face for some familiar features, but my search was vain and I thought that perhaps the unknown woman had been, for me, a chance companion for a few moments. She was clad in showy garments, wearing a silk dress whose hem was frayed, falling over scuffed and distressed minuscule ankle-boots, and beneath an accumulation of withered roses that must have belonged to a hat, her fine red hair was unkempt and tousled. Doubtless I had encountered her one night at the corner of a deserted boulevard and had followed her, but she had fled my memory as dreams flee, and in reality, I never found out how or where she had met me.

"Anselme," she said, "I'm cold."

Those words awoke in me the memory of the warm room that was waiting for me, the bright fire, and I felt myself quiver with an immense and profound pity. She appeared to me as she was, fragile and miserable, prey to the fury of the wind, the dolors of the frost and the rain, trembling with fear and weakness, so dainty and so deprived of energy and strength that it seemed that the nascent morning breeze might carry her away. I was advancing toward her when I saw her eyes dilate in dismay; a great frisson agitated her body; she tottered and would have collapsed on the ground if I had not caught her. I took her in my arms, rang the doorbell, and carried her as far as the third floor like a frail sick child.

In my room I laid her on the low divan near the fire. She slept there until the next day, and the sad smile that she addressed to me when she woke up said that she would like to remain there, in that haven to which destiny had bought her.

She stayed. For months, she lived beside me, and my tenderness for her was made of the pleasure that I experienced in putting her chagrins and her suffering to sleep. I did not feel desire, but a sort of constant compassion, in seeing her curled up by the fire, sitting for long hours on a thick bearskin, while the flames tinted her immobile and silent face pink, plunged in an impenetrable reverie. I watched her, without troubling that repose of her entire body and mind, the repose that she owed to me and by which I felt moved.

As she had not told me her name and I had not wanted to ask her what it was, I called her Annie, and from time to time, when I called her that, she turned her eyes toward me, and it was always the same sad and indecisive smile that I had seen parting her lips on the morning of our encounter that she addressed to me, and which stirred my affectionate pity.

After a time, she changed, emerging from her stupor, like a poor frightened bird that one has picked up in the palm of the hand. She appeared to me less thin, less spectral in appearance, and the pallor of her face was attenuated. She felt herself revive, and she lived. She wandered around the room, brushing each object with the same gesture with which she had brushed my shoulder, still silent but active. Gradually, she began to sing like a bird, and the sad smile of old was replaced by laughter.

As she was transformed, I sensed my tenderness vanishing. Annie embarrassed me, like an intruder; she became an annoyance and an irritation, in hearing her sing and laugh. She was a stranger, it seemed to me, who had come into my home, and no longer a rediscovered sister. As she was very delicate and subtle, she understood the change in me, even though, by virtue of a residue of pity, I tried to hide it from her. What singular idea passed through her childish brain? She thought that the singularity of our fraternal life was irritating me.

It was for that reason that she gave herself to me, and thus she broke the charm; she repaid me for my welcome, and the love that I had felt for her disappeared under her kisses. In the morning, lying beside her, I looked at her as I had looked at her on the day when I took her in my arms; she looked at me too, and I don't know what she saw passing through my eyes, but she got up, and when she had dressed, she extended her hand to me and simply bid me adieu.

I didn't make a gesture to retain her. She left and I never saw her again. Often, pushed by remorse—for as soon as she had quit me I thought about her miserable destiny and all my tenderness overtook me again—I searched for her, but in vain, and sometimes I weep for her, the sweet unknown woman who gave me the egotistical joy of pity.

New Life

AS the shadow took possession of the garden, drowning the bushes and lawns in its folds, Anselme spoke and everyone fell silent in order to listen.

"There are no banal stories," he said, "there are only banal heroes. Any strange or heroic adventure becomes vulgar if those who participated in it and were its actors were of a coarse and insensible nature. Any sequence of events, encountered and disdained a thousand times, appears unique, mysterious and rare for once, if the person who underwent or fell victim to the customary accidents in question had a precious soul, acute senses and refined virtues.

"One can also say that the spirit of the former is like a poor mirror in which images, however beautiful or unexpected they might be, only appears deformed and blurred by fog, denatured and returned to the most abject aspect. The spirit of the latter, on the contrary, is a creative mirror; it gives to every form an incomprehensible and troubling attraction, it is able to extrapolate the lines, to show behind a face the infinity of ideas and sensations to which it is attached; it can, by virtue of the unknown and unsuspected that it adds, embellish and render charming and seductive the phantoms that lean over it.

"It is thus that the life of Étienne Mali acquired, for every individual susceptible of being stirred by the development of the subtlest passions, an inestimable value. It was, however, the most commonplace life that a bourgeois or realist novelist could imagine; it was only valuable by virtue of its extrapolation: its ramifications, if I might put it thus. That life became worthy of curiosity, of sympathy, when it was concluded, when the fundamental, essential events that formed its weave had run out. Then, from their very death, the elements of a new life were born, through which the abolished actions reappeared; from their decrepitude, delicate arborescences issued, taut embroideries, and also harsh arabesques, and finally, peculiar, gracious, terrible and poignant shadows: a gripping cortege of which the mind of a man was the organizer.

"Étienne Mali was a mild young man, inclined to reverie, sad, silent and irresolute. Of delicate intelligence, easily impressionable, he was incapable of resisting the action of beings and things. He submitted, but he was able to submit; he deformed the imprints that he was unable to reject, and his intellectual life was made of those deformations.

"At the age of twenty-five he married a young woman three years his elder, beautiful, passionate, willful, imperious and a little scornful of the man to whom she had given herself. From Hélène—that was her name— he had all joys and all sufferings; she was the passionate microcosm in which his heart agitated.

"He cherished her infinitely; she deceived him; what adventure is more vulgar? She left him; he suffered and waited; she came back; he welcomed her and knew the most bitter jealousies; she died, and he believed that he had reached the final circle of human dolor. Cultivated, nourished on the honey of all literatures and the juice of all philosophies, he did not even have the special satisfaction for which certain refined minds can hope, of being tormented by an exceptional woe. His existence had been commonplace; he could only hope for commonplace anguish.

"When he found himself alone, he was thirsty for solitude. He desired to relive his life, marking its previous stages by means of determination and dreams; he wanted to recover the same jubilations and the same despairs that had marked and staked out his route; he attempted to see nothing alive but the past.

"He retired to the Mediterranean coast, to the depths of an isolated gulf. He lived in a little villa perched on a ridge, a villa crowned with mimosas, perfumed by eucalyptus and lentisks, vibrant with powerful aromas, ornamented with palms and aloes. The gardens of the villa descended in successive stages all the way to a little shingle beach, and the terrace extended in front of the habitation itself overlooked the sea.

"For six months Mali stayed there, with an old woman he had brought with him. No one in the locale knew him, but if he solicited curiosity, he never satisfied it. He never went out of his garden and his housekeeper was mute. One morning, it was learned that he had disappeared; a search was mounted, in vain, and two days later his body was found on the strand.

"When his heirs—two distant cousins—took possession of the furniture in the villa they found a manuscript notebook in the drawer of a work-table. It had been supposed, simply, that Étienne had not wanted to survive the woman he had cherished, and thus had closed in a simultaneously tragic and banal fashion a life which nothing authorized anyone to consider as surprising. The reading of the notebook permitted Mali's friends to revise that opinion, and none of them was able to escape the emotion that the confession of that strangely hallucinated and tormented soul was bound to stimulate.

"I was among Étienne's friends, and no story was ever as dolorous for me as the story of his dreams and visions, of the happiness and the tortures that were for six months the lot of a man who was led to death by them. I cannot publish it in its entirety but I want to extract a few notes that will permit you to judge the dead man, to cherish him, to feel pity for him, and perhaps to envy him.

Tuesday 25 April. I have been here for a month, and this morning, for the first time, I rediscovered Hélène's voice. I was on the beach, leaning against the red rock that the waves were beating, entering into the fissures in the stone and then reemerging with a soft, enticing, voluptuous hiss of surf. The sound resounded within me. It was as if someone had thrown a pebble into the dismal pool of my heart. What secret door did those eddies open? I don't know, but I heard Hélène's living voice.

Thursday 4 May. How the voice has grown since the other day! It's still her, but it is now confounded with the voice of the sea. Hélène's soul is doubtless animating the waves of the gulf.

Friday 5 May. Today the weather is gray and the swell is agitated; clamors are coming from the open sea; it's her voice again, the voice she had in hours of anger and hatred, the voice that once gouged my heart. I live once again the bygone minutes, the desperate minutes in which the appeals of my sobs left her insensible.

Out there, ahead, the waves are rushing against the rocky islet; they really are antique bitches, multiple foaming maws; they're crying out their fury and calling to their lovers. She was as imperious, proud and malevolent as the waves. She was as deceitful and perfidious as the sea. Hélène . . . the sea.

Saturday 3 June. I've seen her today. It was midday, and through the trees, I saw her. Her supple body was bathed in the waves; from the terrace I saw her blue eyes, that dark, profound and ardent blue that searched my senses. She called me and I went down there, but I could no longer see anything but the sea. Doubtless

she had fled. Laughter resounded in the mimosas: the mocking laughter of sirens; her laughter. The sea, which is displaying its foam on the strand, has the form of her body.

✻

Sunday 18 June. I've seen all the days of the past going by in a slow procession. I've found Hélène again. She lives with me and I've reconquered her. The voluptuous body of the sea is Hélène's body. The voice of the waves is definitely her voice, and there are her scintillating pupils; they're the pupils of the water. She has come back, the cruel sea, and the cruel Hélène.

✻

Monday 25 June. She has betrayed me again; she has left me. The sea is dead. Hélene no longer hears my cries.

✻

Friday 29 June. I know that she's still alive, and at dawn I saw her hair on the rocks.

✻

Thursday 5 July. I was bathing, she embraced me. I fainted; she cast me up on the shore, and as I closed my eyes, she said adieu!

✻

Tuesday 10 July. I search for her, I call out to her; my cries are in vain. The air is heavy, as heavy as the silence, as heavy as the sun that is scorching the palm trees.

✳

Sunday 15 July. She hasn't come back. I go down to the beach. The sea is motionless and silent, extending as rigid as a cadaver; my feet beat the water strangely . . . *Hélène is dead* . . . Who said that?

✳

Wednesday 1 August. For a week, a frightful odor has been coming from the sea. It's still mute and lifeless, but out there, near the rocks, it seems to me that green-tinted fissures are furrowing her flesh.

✳

Thursday 9 August. The frightful odor is pursuing me: a terrible perfume of charnel-houses, hallucinating and horrible, a perfume of death; an odor of decaying flesh, an abominable odor of putrescence placed between Hélène and me: the odor of the decomposed sea.

✳

Saturday 11 August. She must be there, in a grotto hollowed out between those rocks, and one morning, she will surge forth before me, her face eaten away, frightful and hideous. I'll find her lying on the and, soft and warm, and that will be my second agony. I won't be able to stand it.

※

Sunday 12 August. Why not join her? Our bodies will be confounded in death, and there will be forgetfulness.

※

Étienne Mali disappeared on 13 August, and two days later his solitary cadaver was lying on the beach.

The Ungraspable Happiness

CERTAIN passions, even unsatisfied, augment the energy of those possessed by them. It is thus with ambition, which manifests itself with all the more force when it has been contained for a long time; it is not the same, in certain cases, with amour. That is because ambition obliges various and multiple actions, which keep the mind awake and stimulate the will able to measure it and magnify it. Amour, on the contrary, in concentrating all aspirations and all steps on a single point, depresses the active being; it wears it away, fascinates it and plunges it, by virtue of the excess of contemplative desire in a dolorous but cherished hypnosis, and leads it to complete impotence. I am speaking, of course, of ambition and amour that have not yet attained their goal and do not possess their object. The capital difference between the two passions is that ambition can always seize the object when it presents itself, while amour sometimes cannot. Several examples of the latter case have been given to me, and I shall tell a story that relates to it.

※

Monsieur de Herloux, whom I knew, was one of the last representatives of the provincial gentry that only recommends itself to the attention of the psychologist or the moralist by virtue of its extreme and naïve vanity. Of that race of men, who compose their society in accordance with a severe code, believing in the privilege of divine right and God's consent to a particular creation of a nobility in the earliest ages of the world.

Monsieur de Herloux was one of the most accomplished specimens. He lived in a little villa in the Lozère, the solitude of which was extremely propitious to the conservation of those once-fundamental prejudices. There, in those mountains, as inaccessible to ideas as to travelers, he vegetated happily, the oracle of a handful of shriveled gentlemen and receiving all the homages that he believed to be due to the descendant of an ancient family.

A widower, Monsieur de Herloux had a son from whom he hoped for nothing as much as to make him the heir of his cockleshell and the principles contained within it. However, that son, Henri had already disconcerted all the projects of paternal affection, and he was able to lead his father, who added him, to what was, for him, the ultimate degree of humiliation.

Henri had a very ordinary youth. He was brought up in a religious house celebrated in the province; he received an excellent education there; he was taught to write Latin verses and given the minimum of conventional ideas necessary even to men of the world. But he was passionate by nature, very tender and very ardent at the same time, timid and capable of resistance, with

a refined but passive mind. Having completed his studies, he returned to live with his father.

Monsieur de Herloux, who cherished him, destined
him for one of his relatives, and dreamed on his behalf
for a customary existence, that of his ancestors and his
own, the existence of a landowning hunter, uniform
and placid, devoid of desires and regrets: a good vegeta-
tive existence shared by a few poor relatives who were
treated with a distant familiarity.

It seemed that nothing ought to raise an obstacle to
such sage projects, Henri even frequented his fiancée
assiduously, thus accustoming himself to her contact,
and he was preparing himself, without enthusiasm and
without difficulty, for the happiness that was promised
to him, when a fortuitous encounter orientated his life
in a very different fashion. In the course of his sylvan
peregrinations, in pursuit of some game, he went into a
farm one day, where he found a numerous company of
excursionists already assembled. Courteously invited,
he took part in the collation offered, and hazard placed
him before a young bourgeois woman from the town.

The interest of this story is not in its beginnings but
in its eventual denouement, so I shall not insist on the
fashion in which the passion that was born that day
was first manifest. It is sufficient for us to know that
Henri became ardently infatuated with Mademoiselle
Lamy—that was the young woman's name. He acted
as all lovers do in that circumstance; he found himself
in the passage of the person he loved, was able one day
to encounter her alone at dusk, told her of his amour,
and, having discovered that it was mutual, experienced
a great joy in consequence.

Everything happened as in the most banal of novels. Henri having resolved to marry his lover, Monsieur de Herloux refused to consent to such a misalliance, and in order to break it off he took his son away.

From then on Henri became a stranger to common life; he created a powerful interior life and lived with the image of the woman he loved; he ornamented her with all the virtues that he would have liked to find in her; he savored in her imaginary company all the pleasures that he would have desired to give her. By the force of his tenderness, he made an idol of his beloved; for him she was all beauty, all intelligence and all joy.

His melancholy was, however, augmented with time; he deteriorated every day, and as the voyage caused him an extreme fatigue, Monsieur le Herloux agreed to return to their homeland. The return journey was such, Henri being prey to a redoubtable nervous anguish, that Monsieur de Herloux became fearful. He reflected for a few days, because it was hard for him to renounce his atavistic vanity, but then, one morning, he went into Henri's room and told him that he consented to his marriage.

At those words, Henri was overtaken by a mortal pallor, and he fainted. When he had recovered his senses his father spoke to him softly, but he could not obtain any response. However, when he asked him whether he wanted to see Mademoiselle Lamy, Henri replied: "It's too late!"

Surprised, Monsieur Herloux asked why, on the threshold of happiness, he refused it, and whether his sentiments in regard to his lover had changed.

"No," he replied, "but I've made of her such an elevated image that I dare not seize her now and make her come to me. She has given me the purest and most perfect satisfactions, she has lived within me in such a fashion that I would fear, in accepting her, only to live with her, and I cannot consent to destroy by my own will what my mind and my heart have edified in anguish and tears. I am grateful to you, however, Father, for having granted me, albeit too late, what was momentarily inestimable for me, and I only ask one thing of your affection: tell my beloved not to weep for my death and not to regret anything, for it is in possessing her that I have lost her."

Those were his last words. He remained motionless all day, his eyes fixed, as if in ecstasy, and he died the same evening. He had doubtless used up all his energy, all his force, in creating his divinity; he no longer sensed sufficient courage within him to support the disillusionment that he foresaw, or that he dreaded, and he died when it was necessary to bring his dream into accord with reality. He was a poor lover, and a weak mind, since he was incapable of operating the conciliation that is the very condition of existence.

The Past in the Present

A NSELME to Nalle.

I have gone, in the life of today, in quest of yesterday, and to seek the soul of long ago that still lies within our present soul. In the Present I wanted to see the Past, and it is for you, who told me once about your horror of that which was no more, that I am writing these pages, day by day, in accordance with the voyage and the encounter.

1. The Soul of the Philosopher

It is necessary to go at dusk through the old quarters of cities, when the light appeases its riot, when the customary noises are extinguished, when the air becomes clearer and lighter. Then, memories awaken more easily, the shadows of old, more familiar, come to prowl around the passer-by, who hears voices dead for a long time and whose echo, at that hour, reverberates in the mind that is prepared to listen to them, for the souls of vanished things and people only haunt the memory of those who love them: they come, shivering, to warm themselves up in the company of those who are able to cherish them.

In cities vibrant with life it is important to choose the moment that announces and prepares for darkness in order to go in search in the midst of the tumult of the pale phantoms of the past, the vagabond procession of which seems, during those brief minutes, to pause in its course and come to rest in places once cherished or detested.

It is thus that, after having wandered for an entire day in Amsterdam, through noisy streets and busy quays, I took refuge, as dusk fell, near the majestic and silent Lord's and Prince's Canals. I followed the tranquil banks, alongside their motionless and somber waters, where, at intervals, flat-bottomed boats lingered that seemed forsaken, and whose silhouettes were reminiscent, in the distance, of great abandoned gondolas. Shiny, profound waters in which the tall houses of merchants were reflected, calm and sad mirrors, contrasted with the other, populous canals cluttered with mercantile flotillas, with surfaces troubled by rudders manipulated by rude boatmen. They surrounded and delimited with their cold lines a few islets of houses asleep in the middle of the noisy city, and as soon as one quits them, one falls back into the agitated crowd filling the length of old Amsterdam with noise.

My reverie and my desires carried me beyond the river, and after having crossed the checkerboard of streets that precedes the Waterlooplein I found myself in the Jewish quarter. There, where the first small group of exiles came to settle in the sixteenth century, a numerous population now swarms. The descendants of the primitive colonists of the "New Jerusalem" celebrated three hundred years ago by Jewish chroniclers and writers have not yet quit the Ghetto that their ancestors founded; every new arrival over the centuries came to establish his hearth in the same place, and only the rich Jews have now forsaken it.

There, one still finds the true Jew, the Jew who believes in his race, in his people, in the power of his rites, in the vitality of his customs, the one who wants to conserve his habits and his mores. There, he is at home, in those tortuous streets, with the muddy ground and the black walls, whose dirtiness contrasts with the cleanliness of the city. The frontons of the houses bear signs ornamented with hieratic characters; shops are hollowed out in damp and repulsive cellars; stalls overflow on to the pavement, laden with the usual bric-a-brac of second-hand dealers.

As the hour is late, the streets and sidewalks are encumbered by the crowd of diamond-cutters and gem-carvers, all Jews, who are quitting the workshops and returning home. It is the ordinary spectacle of the end of the day in an outlying district, to which a few old Jews and a few young women give an exotic and Oriental aspect.

At the western entrance to that Ghetto, in a square, stands a large red brick building; it is the oldest synagogue in Amsterdam, the Portuguese synagogue, which tradition claims to have been built on the plan of the Temple of Jerusalem. I have traversed the courtyard encumbered by a hideous and miserable horde of starvelings, sad wretches whom the wind of persecutions has expelled from Russia or Poland, and whose troop assails visitors deafened and astonished by the clamorous jargon.

After having escaped them I have gone into the still-deserted synagogue and contemplated its décor. Nothing is attractive there: cold woodwork; motionless rows of benches illuminated by copper candleholders placed at intervals on the backs; the platform surrounded by railings where the celebrant stands, to the east, at the back of the edifice; and the ark, very high up, in sandalwood, where the scrolls of the law are enclosed: the habitual house of Jewish prayer, in which the faithful live familiarly with a once-redoubtable God, coming at fixed hours to chat about their affairs with Jehovah or their neighbors. It is not attractive, it is not captivating, and I would have left without having sensed anything alive around me if I had not read, suddenly, on a marble plaque that dates from the foundation of the synagogue in 1679, among the names of the donors, the name of Spinoza, doubtless that of a relative of the great Baruch.

I saw then that it was the shade of the philosopher that had guided me that evening, and I went out in order to go through the back-streets and little squares to live with him for a few more hours. He was born there, in one of those houses that stand on the Burgwal, near a primitive synagogue now destroyed; the little red bricks of the Portuguese temple were its contemporaries. He too wandered through those streets, whose turbulence gave him a taste for solitude.

He had listened to the words of rabbis, and it was on hearing God celebrated that he had conceived the unique substance. Perhaps it was near this crossroads that the man hid one evening whose dagger threatened him, a man who could say, like Saint Paul: "I have been in danger on the part of those of my nation." It was at a spectacle of interested agitations in the crowd of businessmen that he understood the beauty of disinterest and acquired a hatred of money.

I seemed to see him walking in front of me, with his long black curly hair, his emaciated and melancholy face, brown-tinted, with profound and sad eyes, the gentle philosopher who, the target of all anger, never knew anything but the mildness of forgiveness. I never understood more fully that he was not dead, and could not die, that heroic little Jew who had, by means of the power of thought alone, broken the barriers behind which his birth had parked him.

He has left us as an example his perfect life; he has nourished generations on the bread of his ideas. How much closer to me I sensed him, more existent than the population of merchants! It was his soul that animated that corner of the earth, and it is through him that that unsteady soil lived. *He has passed here*, I said to myself, *he has lived, he has suffered, he fled one evening after the anathemas, in order to go and live in peace and meditation, poor, and captivated only by the dream of the eternal essence, and in the midst of all the transitory beings that are crowding around me, it is his shade alone that is real and which is alive, for that shade represents a world.*

2. The Voice of Yesterday

There are cities that only the voice of the Past animates; one might think them dead in the Present; all contemporaneity seems foreign to them, or, at least, they attach the passing moment with those that have disappeared to such a point that the one participates in the apparent life of the others and is drawn into a vague distance that mists blur and dissimulate. Bruges is one of those cities; it is gently asleep on the edge of its canals, in the shadow of its towers and its churches, huddled around its belfry, whose carillon sounds the hours that it can no longer live.

It has a defunct air thus, decked in old clothes, frivolous laces that time has rendered grave, caressed by the joyful wind from the sea, saddened as it passes the ruined gates and runs over the bleak black waters in which the water-lilies seem to be shedding their petals; the wind that seems to unfurl the foliage, chasing away the sedentary water-weeds, ruffling the white plumage of swans and driving back the water in little wavelets, as if it were lifting a heavy mantle.

In reality, it seems quite dead, dead to laughter and dead to ancient splendors, but, like its peers, it permits the delicious and inexpressible pleasure of coming alive again, of reanimating, of populating itself with laughter and songs, corteges and cavalcades: a pleasure comparable to that which legendary princes must have experienced when they woke young virgins asleep for centuries in old abandoned castles. To know that joy, it is sufficient to walk around Bruges, to walk slowly through the streets that grass has tinted green, to sit down near its bell-towers, to haunt its naves and crypts, to lean on sepulchers that bear the names of the Téméraire and Marie and to meditate in subterranean chapels.[1]

But a precious corner exists in which one can sense and hear olden times completely, a corner where the feeble heart of Bruges beats. It is the little square where the Basilica of the Holy Blood and the Hôtel de Ville stand, which was the cradle of the city, the place where the primitive burg was born. From that square one can see the tower of the belfry, and all Bruges is there. It is the mystical Bruges, austerely religious, crudely pious, like the unique, primitive and rudimentary sculpture that ornaments the fronton of the ruined and desolate chapel of Baudouin Bras-de-Fer, and it is the Bruges of communicants and merchants, rude and turbulent métiers, opulent and proud traffickers.

For Bruges was not only the city of flowers of dream, of the lilies of the faith, the roses of piety, the city of gentle and sad virgins, of saints whose hands were raised in chalices, women always desolated by the incessantly renewed death of Christ. It was a joyful port, doubtless full of licentious songs, a cosmopolitan port in which thirty-four nations rubbed shoulders. The crossroads, bleak today, were animated by the coarse gaiety of sailors on the spree, drunk on beer and running after whores, invading the taverns that are dormant now, for the drinkers there speak in low tones and their voices have echoes under the vaults.

---

1 Marie de Bourgogne (1457-1482), the daughter of Charles le Téméraire (1433-1477) died in Bruges and was buried in Notre-Dame-de-Bruges.

When the Reye, free and noisy, brought the wind of the sea all the way to the main square, now deserted, Bruges was a caravanserai of peoples, and the riches of the Occident and the Orient piled up in its warehouses. Its quays were frequented by Swedes and Russians, Armenians and Tartars, Moroccans and Jerusalemites. Under the vaults of the Waterhalle, all languages resounded; trade was conducted in all tongues, and like all Babels of peoples, like all international cities of negotiations, Bruges must have been extremely dissolute. We know that it was sumptuous, for legends remain of the women of Bruges who excited the jealousy of Jeanne de Navarre. It was also a city of proud and hard merchants, and in the portraits painted by Gérard David and Pieter Pourbus one can still find them.

At the Holy Blood, one sees them as they ought to be, the members of the Brotherhood, perpetuated by Pourbus. They have the dry and rugged faces of men who regard as serfs all those who work with their hands, and at the same time they have the satisfied expression of men whose coffers are full, whose warehouses are overflowing and for whom the artisans, the little people, work. Even now, that expression marks the faces of their descendants, who inscribe on their doors, below their name, the simple word *koopman*: merchant.

However, such as they are and such as they were, they cannot forget everything that has illuminated Bruges, everything that has been the art of the Van Eycks and the Memlings, and it is in the paintings of those old and marvelous masters that the duality of Bruges is synthesized.

That is where the life of Bruges is. It is because it is entirely a museum that it is not dead, that, on the contrary, it lives powerfully, superlatively. It is one of those incomparable cities, like Arles and Nuremberg, in the middle of which one conceives that the past is not always a skeleton, and it is only there and in our minds that it appears among us alive and young. The museums of great cities, of Paris, Munich, Berlin, Florence and London, give the impression of necropolises; it is necessary, in their galleries, to make a powerful effort to be able to find, beneath the varnish of canvases, flesh, blood, passion and intelligence; it is necessary to resuscitate the dead. In Bruges, that is not the case. The ambiance prepares us or that confrontation with olden times, it leads us to penetrate it; on our soul of today it superimposes another soul, and we are then in the admirable state that that permits us to link the present hour and the hour gone by, to savor both simultaneously, in their differences, and, above all, in their analogies. A precious thing! For that analogy of yesterday with today is the very breath that keeps it alive.

Let us go see Van Eyck and Hans Memling, then. We have seen them in the Louvre, at the Pinakothek in Munich, in the museum of Berlin, but never, doubtless, will we sense them as we can here, in the small rooms of the Saint John's Hospital and the museum. And it is not so much Van Eyck as Memling who is dear to us, for the latter appears to us more perfectly, his example is finer and more complete, and it is in him that we grasp better the duality of Bruges that we mentioned just now.

That German, who was doubtless born in Mimlingen, near Mayence, synthesizes the inhabitants of Bruges, an excellent representation of the soul of the city, a soul that is similar to the diptychs of its painter, and if he incarnates it to that degree it is because he was not born there. Bruges was not his homeland, but it was the one he chose, because his sentiments and his thought were in harmony with it. He had chosen it because it was veritably his land, the land that was not imposed on him by tradition, habits or prejudices, the land of his free selection. Thus, it is Master Hans, the German, who is the inhabitant of Bruges *par excellence*: with an irony made to disconcert nationalists and narrow patriots, it is that foreigner who has best grasped the spirit of the city, to which nothing attached him—not family, education, costume or atavistic sentiments. He is the one who ought to be our guide, and he is the one we ought to follow in order to understand the living and the dead who were their forefathers.

There, in Saint John's Hospital, where bloodless beings—invalids or nuns—are wandering under the low arches, how one understands mystical Bruges and mercantile Bruges! Here are the slender virgins leaning over like excessively heavy flowers: there a Catherine surprised and raped; Ursula ready for martyrdom; a naïve Herodias, simultaneously smiling, astonished and satisfied, whose figures on the right-hand shutter of the Mystical Marriage of Saint Catherine of Alexandria, a mild and slightly perverse Herodias, whose eyes are astonished by the crime her mouth has ordered; and there is Mary weeping at the foot of Calvary and Magdalen with the swollen eyes and the quivering bosom. The entire flower of the candid religious dream blooms again in that little rectangular room where one regrets seeing a Van Dyck above the mantelpiece of sculpted wood.

But alongside those saints and legendary heroines, to the right and the left, on diptychs and triptychs, are the donors: the authoritarians, the hierarchical merchants. They are alive, on the wood that time has fractured; we saw them just now wandering through the streets, and again in doorways; we find them again here, and we can understand them, even now that the sea, by withdrawing its waves, which enter the city by way of the gentle Minnewater, has left death on the shores that it vivified.

On the two shutters that represent the Virgin and Child to the right and the burgomaster Martin van Nieuwenhoven to the left, one sees mystical faith and mercantile utilitarianism brought into accord. Martin must have been a shrewd merchant, but he was able to reconcile his practicality in business with his devout ardor, and on the profits conquered from the humble or rivals he levied the tithe that was to preserve the favors of Heaven for him. His descendants still think the same way; they have not changed in four hundred years, but they only have reality in the paintings of Master Hans, and it is all that there is of the living in Memling's painting that brings us close to the defunct city, for the past only pleases us when we feel its palpitating around us and it only consents to brush us with its wing when we are able to love it.

✳

3. The Death of the Waters

Certain adventures of souls are only worthwhile by virtue of the décor in which they are situated. They are commentated, if not necessitated, by the milieu in which they unfold and from which they cannot be removed. That would isolate them, or at least render them less perfect; that is why, before telling the story of Gros de Quellène, it is necessary to evoke the place where he lived.

When one leaves Bruges via the old basins where a few boats with flat bottoms and green-tinted hulls are asleep, if one follows the canal that leads to the port of Dame, one arrives—after three hours of walking, during which one follows the bank through meadows extending to the right and left—at a town lost in the midst of grasslands, a placed of silence and death: that is Sluys, the Sluice-Gate, a cadaver of a town extended in the polders.

Few places in the world give such an impression of neglect and abandonment. The waves of the canal come to expire in the cul-de-sac of a deserted quay, around which placid houses are accumulated. No sound extends there except the bell of the little railway that goes toward Breskens; and the insipid odor of stagnant water adds to the illusion that one is in a town deprived of life. Nevertheless, one does not sense there the invasion of the sadness that pricks us when, after having passed through the streets of the defunct burg, one comes to wander along the high green banks that surround it. They were once the ramparts of Sluys, and one sees them extend their ditches, their steep slopes and their circumvolutions, where cows now graze, and anguish grips the heart at the thought of what that mummified village once was.

The sea once came to batter those walls; the waves of the Zwyn extended there; the deserted quay was a magnificent harbor, to which the ships of nations came bearing the spices, golden cloth, rare metals and furs that were piled up in the warehouses on which shone the eagle of the Komtoor of Bruges. There, in the present meadows, battles were fought; ships collided, and if one dug deep in this soil, one would doubtless find ornate prows buried there.

One day, the living waves withdrew; henceforth, they were only seen from the top of the great windmill or the tower; they unfurl in the distance, where a silver line is perceptible, cut by a brown patch—Zeeland—and the earth they vivified has no more breath. But it took many years to die, years during which the sea combated the sands that it brought. I have found the story of someone who lived in the epoch of that agony, and his memory in that decrepitude has been more violent than the spectacle of the present abandonment.

His name was Gros de Quellène. He was witness to the terrors of the ocean, he witnessed its convulsions; he acquired a profound, unfortunate and inevitable taste for that death, the image of which he constantly had before his eyes.

He was an aristocrat of mild, sad and anxious humor; he had traveled a great deal in his youth and had only returned to Sluys, where he was born, when he was past thirty. He lived there for a few years quietly enough, devoting himself to music, taking pleasure in Italian songs, because he knew that language perfectly, and even composed sonnets; he liked paintings very much, and several of the best painters in Flanders worked for him.

At the age of forty he married. No one knows why, and it surprised everyone. He was thought to be little inclined to matters of amour, and a few young men even said, although without malevolence and without proof, that he was unfeeling. He married the daughter of a merchant of Bruges who was very rich; her name was Françoise Ondvelde, and she had a reputation in the region for beauty. She was, in fact, a very beautiful person, tall and strong, a robust Fleming, with slightly ponderous charms.

Once married, they lived happily without testifying to one another an extraordinary passion. He did not seem to be infatuated with her, nor she with him; she was a loyal wife, attached to her duty, not because she put nothing above it, but because she had been taught what was required of her. As for Gros, he was neither a discourteous nor an unfaithful husband; he was, Françoise said, very good to her, but he demanded that she never leave him alone.

After three years of marriage, Françoise died while giving birth to a dead child. Gros de Quellène showed himself to be extremely contrite, and observed a very strict mourning. A year after the death of Françoise, however, it was learned, not without further astonishment, that he was to marry again. This time he married a young woman from Sluys by the name of Catherine Ostade.

Catherine Ostade was the living antithesis of Françoise; she was petite, slender seemingly fragile and unhealthy; she had a prominent forehead and bulging eyes, very long arms and hands, and large ears that stuck out somewhat from her head. Her humor was taciturn; she haunted churches and prayed a great deal. She agreed to be Quellène's wife because she knew his character to be melancholy and somber.

During the first months of their union, she savored a mild and profound peace; she lived as a wife as she had lived as a young woman, and her spouse did not oppose either her tastes or her habits. It seemed that that happy existence ought never to be troubled, and it would not have been, if a strange malady had not gripped Gros de Quellène.

Having always lived reclusively, he suddenly began to neglect his home. He went out at dawn and only returned late at night. He left the town and went toward the sea, through the cumulating sands that were stifling the port. When he arrived in the vicinity of the surf, he lay down on the strand, with his ear to the ground, and stayed there all day, sometimes soliloquizing but more often listening, mutely, to the sounds that, for him, ran along the beach.

His wife wanted to go with him and, taking pity on him, asked to sit down nearby and not to abandon him. For the first time since he had married her he flew into a temper and chased her away, saying that her presence prevented him from hearing the last breaths of the Zwyn, which was dying. Catherine drew away, but she kept watch on the unfortunate from a distance, because she feared that his folly might lead to some extremity.

However, he did not want to kill himself, and she saw that clearly, for a singular passion invaded him.

He said that he was in love with the sea, and he wandered along the shore declaiming the sonnets that he had once amused himself in composing. He often interrupted himself in order to speak to her in verse, and he made long speeches to her. He said that he loved the sea because she was no longer powerful and redoubtable, that he cherished her for her terrors, for her death-throes, that he adored her for the perfume of death that she spread over the fields and the town, the acrid, terrible perfume that gripped the flesh all the way to the marrow of the bones, for the penetrating and floating odor of neglect that the mist threw over the sand, the sand that quivered like a dying body.

His dementia was augmented by his speeches. Soon, the sea took on for him a known form; in evoking it like a dead woman, he saw surging before him the person who had had his initial tenderness, and it was under the features of Françoise Ondvelde that the dying sea appeared to him. From then on he began to love passionately the woman for whom he had not wept as copiously on the day she disappeared. Death, at that time, ornamented her with a thousand charms that he had not known; he recreated her in accordance with a new dream, a marvelous dream born of the depths of the decomposed ocean whose shores he had haunted for months, and again he came to cloister himself in the solitude of his dwelling, bringing his amour with him.

He lived thus for ten years, alone with the dead woman whom his mysterious madness had resuscitated. He never wanted to see his wife any longer. Catherine's face horrified him; her voice expelled the chimera with which he wanted to live, and which he guarded jealously.

In spite of everything, Catherine did not abandon him; she did not want to deliver his dementia to the brutality of servants who would not have understood its beauty. She remained with him, without showing herself, and when he died she respected his last wish, which was to be buried alongside Françoise.

Thus, in the midst of those ruins, in those fields perfumed by salt, which seem incapable even of reanimating a dream, I have been able nevertheless to live with vanished beings, I have made their troubles, their suffering and their joys mine. I have conceived that similar spirits might still live today, experiencing the same sentiments, groaning in the same impotence, and that that drama could be played out in a contemporary city that the great inconstant, the sea, had resolved to neglect.

That is the way that what there is of the living in the past grips us; that which is dead—its laws, its customs, its mores—might interest us, but cannot seduce us; for that we need know its thought and its passion.

4. The North Sea

I wanted to see the living sea, and I have come to a village that is not haunted by any memory. I arrived yesterday, at night. This morning, from my room in the inn, I hear her, the great sea whose profound voice expands beyond the strand, and I go toward her across the fields.

On quitting Bruges, whose canals embrace an agonizing water that seemed green-tinted by the death of its own molecules, after having rested in the meadows of Sluys, I had the desire to see her, the eternal rebel whose free swell is never appeased, whose appeal rises above human clamors, to extract us from age-old chains and conduct us to where no one can bind us.

Now that I sense her nearby, however, that I can hear her speech, that I perceive her counsel and divine her mysteries and austere lessons, I dally, taking the longest route, doubtless in order to prepare myself to see her, to collect myself and come to weight my thoughts before the entity that was the generatrice of multiple forms, the womb of beings and the ancestress of humankind.

Behind the village, I have taken a path passing close to the church, which is surrounded and guarded by peaceful tombs. It follows a small verdant crest; to the left, the plain extends, to the right, the dunes, and further away, on the horizon, the meadows and the steeple of Sluys. Soon, however, the path descends slightly and I have nothing around me but the plain and the dunes, the romantic and living contrast of the joy of festivals confounding with the melancholy of solitudes.

That is the attraction of this terrain, and I think about that while walking. Just now, on the other side of a bank, I saw a little girl with a prominent forehead, a vague and veiled gaze, and now there are robust Fleming women cutting wheat, who salute me as I pass by, and it pleases me not to understand what they are saying, for I imagine other things that they might be. The little girl and the women whose grating sickles I can hear cutting down the ears are the double image of this race and this region.

Many have sought the spirit that animates different soils, and the soul that haunts them; they have attempted to find the unique breath that vivifies and elevates them, and they have deceived themselves in that search for unity. Human being is double, even multiple, but it is not alone in that; every corner of the world is multiform, inhabited by dissimilar spirits, and the children of each region orientate themselves in accordance with their nature; they listen to the voices that their ears can hear especially, and thus oppose themselves to one another in a simple fashion, permitting them to be divided into neat categories that correspond to the various souls of the native land.

Here, I can only discern at present the two poles, the crude dualist division: the lush fields covered with crops and pasturage with thick grass, opposed to the sterile dunes. I go alongside the fields and meadows, which a soft and blond light envelops with profound and fat colors; everything seems to be full of moisture; the eye reposes on the pastures interrupted here and there by clumps of flexible trees, houses with red roofs, sometimes coated in pale pink or light blue; at intervals, there are windmills whose sails are turning silently.

It is a landscape of sturdy, tranquil joy, communicating the desire to abandon oneself to the sensations that assail like a broad and placid blade, a cheerful and sleepy landscape in which one can image joyful, singing corteges and tables under the foliage. In order to impregnate myself with that wellbeing I pause near a farm, whose garden is florid with an army of proud sunflowers; cows are lying near the road, ruminating, raising their muzzles now and again in order to sniff the sea mist. The perfume of spray is floating in the air; that is what extracts me from the invasive torpor. I abandon the plain, and it is through the dunes that I am now going.

They extend their dirty gray mounds, the forms of which are as supple as bodily forms. Here and there, clumps of long thin grass stain their flanks; short and velvety lawns are designed in the minuscule valleys. In spite of the grass, however, and in spite of a few scrawny bushes, they seem naked, and it is of that nudity that their melancholy is made.

My feet sink into the sand, which is warm, and I wander at hazard, going straight ahead toward the sea, which is still calling. Around me I can no longer see anything; there is a forceful solitude, and I feel alone. Then I lie back against a hillock and I listen, for it is now, when the sand surrounds you, that one hears the master and king of the dunes: the wind. It comes from the sea, where it moans, and it is divided; it surrounds each hillock, enlaces all of them; its thousand mouths kiss them, it strips them, and sometimes covers them; it insinuates itself between the blades of grass, whistles with its thousands of lips: a long, intense whistle, often punctuated by a dull click. Then, when it has visited its domain thus, it rises above it, and travels with great wing-beats, soaring high; its harmonies are reinforced, aggravating, and, suddenly, it drops, in order to permit the song of the surf to reach me.

I could spend hours like that, if, in front of me, beyond the dune, I could not smell the sea; and I escape the wind, attracted by the divine sadness, and climb the last rampart.

I am standing on the summit; the soft white sand flows like a soft carpet of felt toward the beach, and there, facing, extending to infinity, majestic, powerful, redoubtable and benevolent, is the North Sea, which is tender and seductive this morning. An immense, profound and gentle peace invades me. As I stand on the ridge where I am, deaf to any speech that is not that of the waters, it seems to me that I am about to be annihilated in her. I think about days gone by, the shades with which I have come to live, and I believe that I am their contemporary.

Behold the eternal sea: what was yesterday, and what is today, when one compares them before her, and does not everything recombine in order to dissolve and reunite? The past and the present? A voice that emerges from the surf tells me that they are a single living point in eternity.

A PARTIAL LIST OF SNUGGLY BOOKS

G. ALBERT AURIER *Elsewhere and Other Stories*
S. HENRY BERTHOUD *Misanthropic Tales*
LÉON BLOY *The Desperate Man*
LÉON BLOY *The Tarantulas' Parlor and Other Unkind Tales*
ÉLÉMIR BOURGES *The Twilight of the Gods*
JAMES CHAMPAGNE *Harlem Smoke*
FÉLICIEN CHAMPSAUR *The Latin Orgy*
FÉLICIEN CHAMPSAUR
    The Emerald Princess and Other Decadent Fantasies
BRENDAN CONNELL *Clark*
BRENDAN CONNELL *Unofficial History of Pi Wei*
RAFAELA CONTRERAS *The Turquoise Ring and Other Stories*
ADOLFO COUVE *When I Think of My Missing Head*
QUENTIN S. CRISP *Aiaigasa*
QUENTIN S. CRISP *Graves*
LADY DILKE *The Outcast Spirit and Other Stories*
CATHERINE DOUSTEYSSIER-KHOZE *The Beauty of the Death Cap*
ÉDOUARD DUJARDIN *Hauntings*
BERIT ELLINGSEN *Now We Can See the Moon*
BERIT ELLINGSEN *Vessel and Solsvart*
ENRIQUE GÓMEZ CARRILLO *Sentimental Stories*
EDMOND AND JULES DE GONCOURT *Manette Salomon*
REMY DE GOURMONT *From a Faraway Land*
GUIDO GOZZANO *Alcina and Other Stories*
EDWARD HERON-ALLEN *The Complete Shorter Fiction*
RHYS HUGHES *Cloud Farming in Wales*
J.-K. HUYSMANS *Knapsacks*
COLIN INSOLE *Valerie and Other Stories*
JUSTIN ISIS *Pleasant Tales II*
JUSTIN ISIS (**editor**) *Marked to Die: A Tribute to Mark Samuels*
JUSTIN ISIS AND DANIEL CORRICK (**editors**)
    Drowning in Beauty: The Neo-Decadent Anthology

9 781645 250272